"Let me go!" Angelique shouted. "I don't have anything else to say to you!"

"Not a chance." Day dragged her back into the truck, and her frantic clutch for the door handle slammed the door shut. When he realized he had a lapful of woman, he chuckled.

The sound must have infuriated her, because she twisted and wriggled twice as frantically. "Damn you, Day Kincaid. I'm not one of your heifers to be wrestled into submission. I don't want to talk to you!"

He felt his temper beginning to fray at the edges. As she struggled, one hand came up and smacked him solidly in the chest. That did it. Capturing that hand and her other one, which was about to make contact with his jaw, he gritted, "Okay, you don't want to talk, we won't talk."

And then he crushed his lips down on hers....

Dear Reader,

Welcome to Silhouette Desire! This month, we have something special in store for you—book #1 of the *new* Silhouette miniseries, ALWAYS A BRIDESMAID! In ALWAYS A BRIDESMAID! you'll get to read how five women get the men of their dreams. Each book will be featured in a different Silhouette series…one book a month beginning this month with *The Engagement Party* by Barbara Boswell.

In addition, we've got a wonderful MAN OF THE MONTH by award-winning author Jennifer Greene called *Single Dad*. Josh is a hero you'll never forget.

Don't miss *Dr. Daddy*, book #3 in Elizabeth Bevarly's series FROM HERE TO MATERNITY. And a new series, WEDDING BELLES, by Carole Buck launches with the charming *Annie Says I Do*.

A book by Jackie Merritt is always a treat, and she's sure to win new fans—and please her present admirers— with *Hesitant Husband*. And Anne Marie Winston's *Rancher's Wife* completes what I feel is a perfect month!

Silhouette Desire—you've just got to read them all!

Enjoy!

Lucia Macro
Senior Editor

Please address questions and book requests to:
Silhouette Reader Service
U.S.: 3010 Walden Ave., P.O. Box 1325, Buffalo, NY 14269
Canadian: P.O. Box 609, Fort Erie, Ont. L2A 5X3

You're About to Become a *Privileged Woman.*

INTRODUCING
PAGES & PRIVILEGES™.

It's our way of thanking you for buying
our books at your favorite retail store.

— *GET ALL THIS FREE* —
WITH JUST ONE PROOF OF PURCHASE:

◆ Hotel Discounts up to 60% at home and abroad

◆ Travel Service - Guaranteed lowest published
  airfares plus 5% cash back on tickets

◆ $25 Travel Voucher

◆ Sensuous Petite Parfumerie collection ($50 value)

◆ Insider Tips Letter with sneak previews of
  upcoming books

◆ Mystery Gift (if you enroll before 6/15/95)

You'll get a FREE personal card, too.
It's your passport to all these benefits— and to
even more great gifts & benefits to come!

There's no club to join. No purchase commitment. No obligation.

As a *Privileged Woman,*
you'll be entitled to all these *Free Benefits.* And *Free Gifts,* too.

To thank you for buying our books, we've designed an exclusive FREE program called *PAGES & PRIVILEGES*™. You can enroll with just one Proof of Purchase, and get the kind of luxuries that, until now, you could only read about.

*B*IG HOTEL DISCOUNTS

A privileged woman stays in the finest hotels. And so can you—at up to 60% off! Imagine standing in a hotel check-in line and watching as the guest in front of you pays $150 for the same room that's only costing you $60. Your *Pages & Privileges* discounts are good at Sheraton, Marriott, Best Western, Hyatt and thousands of other fine hotels all over the U.S., Canada and Europe.

*F*REE DISCOUNT TRAVEL SERVICE

A privileged woman is always jetting to romantic places. When you fly, just make one phone call for the lowest published airfare at time of booking—or double the difference back! PLUS—

you'll get a $25 voucher to use the first time you book a flight AND 5% cash back on every ticket you buy thereafter through the travel service!

𝒻REE GIFTS!

A privileged woman is always getting wonderful gifts.

Luxuriate in rich fragrances that will stir your senses (and his). This gift-boxed assortment of fine perfumes includes three popular scents, each in a beautiful designer bottle. <u>Truly Lace</u>...This luxurious fragrance unveils your sensuous side. <u>L'Effleur</u>...discover the romance of the Victorian era with this soft floral. <u>Muguet des bois</u>...a single note floral of singular beauty. This $50 value is yours—FREE when you enroll in *Pages & Privileges*! And it's just the beginning of the gifts and benefits that will be coming your way!

𝒻REE INSIDER TIPS LETTER

A privileged woman is always informed. And you'll be, too, with our free letter full of fascinating information and sneak previews of upcoming books.

𝓜ORE GREAT GIFTS & BENEFITS TO COME

A privileged woman always has a lot to look forward to. And so will you. You get all these wonderful FREE gifts and benefits now with only one purchase...and there are no additional purchases required. However, each additional retail purchase of Harlequin and Silhouette books brings you a step closer to even more great FREE benefits like half-price movie tickets...and even more FREE gifts like these beautiful fragrance gift baskets:

L'Effleur ...This basketful of romance lets you discover L'Effleur from head to toe, heart to home.

Truly Lace ...A basket spun with the sensuous luxuries of Truly Lace, including Dusting Powder in a reusable satin and lace covered box.

𝓔NROLL 𝒩OW!
Complete the Enrollment Form on the back of this card and become a Privileged Woman today!

Enroll Today in *PAGES & PRIVILEGES*™, the program that gives you Great Gifts and Benefits with just one purchase!

Enrollment Form

☐ *Yes!* I WANT TO BE A *P*RIVILEGED *W*OMAN.

Enclosed is one *PAGES & PRIVILEGES*™ Proof of Purchase from any Harlequin or Silhouette book currently for sale in stores (Proofs of Purchase are found on the back pages of books) and the store cash register receipt. Please enroll me in *PAGES & PRIVILEGES*™. Send my Welcome Kit and FREE Gifts -- and activate my FREE benefits -- immediately.

NAME (please print)

ADDRESS   APT. NO

CITY   STATE   ZIP/POSTAL CODE

▼ DETACH HERE AND MAIL TODAY! ▼

PROOF OF PURCHASE

**NO CLUB!
NO COMMITMENT!**
Just one purchase brings you great Free Gifts and Benefits!
(See inside for details.)

Please allow 6-8 weeks for delivery. Quantities are limited. We reserve the right to substitute items. Enroll before October 31, 1995 and receive one full year of benefits.

Name of store where this book was purchased_____

Date of purchase_____

Type of store:

☐ Bookstore   ☐ Supermarket   ☐ Drugstore

☐ Dept. or discount store (e.g. K-Mart or Walmart)

☐ Other (specify)_____

Which Harlequin or Silhouette series do you usually read?

_____

Complete and mail with one Proof of Purchase and store receipt to:

U.S.: *PAGES & PRIVILEGES*™, P.O. Box 1960, Danbury, CT 06813-1960

Canada: *PAGES & PRIVILEGES*™, 49-6A The Donway West, P.O. 813, North York, ON M3C 2E8   **PRINTED IN U.S.A**

ANNE MARIE WINSTON
RANCHER'S WIFE

SILHOUETTE *Desire*

Published by Silhouette Books

America's Publisher of Contemporary Romance

SILHOUETTE BOOKS

ISBN 0-373-05936-1

RANCHER'S WIFE

ANNE MARIE WINSTON

A native Pennsylvanian and former educator, Anne Marie is a book lover, an animal lover and always a teacher at heart. She and her husband have two daughters and a menagerie of four-footed family members. When she's not parenting, writing or reading, she devotes her time to a variety of educational efforts in her community. Readers can write to Anne Marie at P.O. Box 302, Zullinger, PA 17272.

For Katrina...
I love you, Bean

One

"Hello. My name is Angel." Angelique Sumner Vandervere closed the door of the dark blue rental car she'd driven out to the Red Arrow Ranch. Smiling, she surveyed the child before her.

The small girl stood at the top of the steps fronting the porch on the big farmhouse. A disreputable white blanket draped over her shoulder and the thumb of the hand that clutched the blanket was tucked firmly in her mouth. Black curls tumbled about her shoulders and wide eyes regarded Angel solemnly. The fingers of her other hand brushed idly back and forth across the ruff of a scruffy-looking black-and-white dog. The dog wasn't bothering to look friendly, Angel noted, watching his lip curl up to reveal shining white canine teeth.

The little one was dressed in a light cotton shift, perfect clothing for a hot July day in southwestern New Mexico. In contrast, Angel felt hot and grubby in her two-piece traveling suit.

"I'm here to visit Dulcie Meadows," she said to the child. "Do you know her?"

The little girl nodded shyly from behind the thumb. Beside her, the dog gave a menacing snarl.

Enchanted, Angel ignored the animal and tried again. "Can you find her for me?"

A grin slowly spread behind the thumb but the child made no move.

Angel might have been exasperated but the little girl was so adorable she couldn't summon up any irritation. The child looked to be about three, and a piercing pain smote her as she made the inevitable association. Emmie was five now, soon to be six. What Angel wouldn't give to be this close to Emmie, even for a single minute!

Deliberately she pulled her mind back to the present, recoiling from the grief and regret. No sense in crying over what she couldn't change, she told herself firmly. Digging into her purse, she withdrew one of the candies she always popped into her mouth when her flights took off and landed. "Would you like a piece of candy?"

The child nodded. The thumb stayed in her mouth as she reached for the candy with the other small hand.

"Beth Ann! No!"

The sharp masculine command made both Angel and the child jump. Angel's hand jerked and the candy fell to the dusty ground. As she looked around for the source of the voice, a cowboy—a *big* cowboy—wearing a black hat, crossed the porch from a side door in two quick strides. Reaching for the little girl, he swung her protectively into his arms. Then he straightened and turned to face Angel as she stood, frozen in puzzlement and rising outrage.

"Get off my land," he said, and his tone was deep and menacing. As menacing as the black brows that drew together over hooded eyes shot with dark flames of rage.

He was broad shouldered, deep chested, taller than she by several inches, even in her heels. She had to squash the involuntary leap of fear produced by his aggressive attitude. "I'm sorry if somehow I've offended—"

But he didn't give her a chance to complete the sentence. Setting the child down, the cowboy stepped forward. One big hand shot out and snared her upper arm in an unbreakable grip. Before she could utter a protest, he was literally dragging her back toward her car. Behind him, the dog set up a sharp, vicious barking.

Angel stiffened her legs, seeking purchase on the rough ground, though all that did was ensure that the heels of her expensive leather pumps bumped and scuffed over the earth. Reality receded and the fear she'd succeeded in subduing for weeks suddenly rushed over her. The thing she feared more than anything in the world was happening.

The man—the faceless, nameless one from whom she was running—had found her.

Fear endowed her with exceptional strength. She leaned away, then slammed herself hard against him, banging her head painfully against his chin. He yelped and swore but his hands didn't loosen. She twisted her body, wriggling and writhing in his grasp, but after the first surprised instant, her efforts appeared to have less than no effect.

"Let me go," she gasped as he plowed to a halt beside her car. Her voice sounded breathless and ineffective, even to her.

"Get off my land," he said again. He had both her arms now and he shook her after every few syllables as if to emphasize his words. "Nobody is taking my child away from me ever again. You can go straight back to Jada and tell her—"

"Day, stop!"

The familiar voice of her childhood friend was a welcome relief to Angel. This was all some sort of horrible mistake. She immediately relaxed her body. And was sorry a moment later as her determined attacker yanked open the door of the rental car and slammed her forcefully into the driver's seat.

"Ooph!" The air whooshed from her lungs and she fell forward over the steering wheel, gasping for breath.

"David Kincaid, you stop bullying Angel at once." Dulcie's voice came again, steely anger replacing the mild reproof in her tones. In her peripheral vision, Angel could see her friend hurrying forward, unceremoniously shoving the big cowboy out of her way. "If you would have asked before performing your caveman feats, you might have learned that she's going to be my guest at this ranch."

The big man merely folded his arms and stood where he'd planted himself as Dulcie helped Angel from the car. As he glared at her, the dark suspicion didn't ease even a fraction. "You didn't tell me you invited someone to visit," he said to Dulcie. It was almost an accusation.

"I didn't realize I needed your permission," Dulcie countered. "I'm here at the Red Arrow, in which we share ownership, to do you a favor. You'd do well to remember it." Unfazed by his grim expression, she examined Angel anxiously. "Are you all right?"

Angel nodded. "More or less." She smiled wryly, hoping to defuse the tense moment. "Maybe I should begin again."

Dulcie's understanding grin highlighted her dark, sultry beauty. She stepped forward with both arms spread wide, mimicking surprise. "Angel, welcome to the Red Arrow. It's great to see you!"

Angel laughed at the silly pretense, hugging her shorter friend. "It's great to see you, too. As usual, it's been too long."

"Have you met my brother?" Dulcie's courtesy had a distinct edge to it when she turned to wave a hand in the direction of the man who still stood behind her, unsmiling. "Angel, my brother, Day Kincaid, older than me by enough years to make him incredibly bossy. Day, this is

Angel Vandervere. Angel is a friend of mine from high school. She doesn't live around here anymore, and I invited her to spend some time with me while I'm at the ranch.''

Angel held out her hand and took a deep breath, determined to get past the awkward moment. Angel Vandervere, not her stage name, Angelique Sumner. Though she assumed Day Kincaid recognized her face from her movies, she was grateful to Dulcie for emphasizing her need for privacy. ''It's nice to meet you,'' she murmured.

He didn't take the offered hand, merely nodded his head once in a curt gesture. ''How long will you be staying, Miss Vandervere?''

''I asked her to stay for two weeks,'' Dulcie inserted before she could respond. Then the smaller woman addressed Angel again. ''I apologize for my brother's unfriendliness earlier. Day thought you were someone his ex-wife hired to kidnap my niece.''

She knew her eyes widened in shock. That explained his behavior. It didn't excuse it, she decided, rubbing her arm where her elbow and the car door had had a forceful encounter. But it certainly did explain it. A bubble of slightly hysterical, relieved laughter rose in her throat and she hastily cut it short. After the strain and fear she'd been under for the past few months, she'd looked forward to getting away from L.A. and seeing Dulcie again. How hilarious! That she should be attacked the moment she set foot on New Mexican soil.

The urge to laugh died abruptly as a movement on the porch caught her eye. ''I believe your daughter needs some reassurance, Mr. Kincaid,'' she said. The sight of the little girl, who was now cowering behind one of the porch posts, lent a decided coolness to her tone. ''You appear to have terrified someone other than me.''

''You should know better than to offer candy to a child you don't know,'' he retorted. ''If she's terrified, it's your fault. Candy is an invitation most children can't resist. If she takes it from a stranger who turns out to be a friend, then how am I supposed to make her understand it could be dangerous?'' Without giving her a chance to reply, he turned away, walking over to lift his daughter into his arms again.

Angel stared at Day's retreating back as he vanished into the house with the little girl. ''Wow. He's certainly prickly.''

Dulcie gave a rueful sigh. ''That's my brother—dripping with charm.'' She gave Angel another concerned once-over. ''Are you really all right? From where I stood, it looked as if he was being pretty rough.''

''He was, but I'll survive.''

Dulcie seemed about to comment further, then apparently thought better of it. ''I can't believe you're finally here. But you look tired. Why don't I show you where your room is and you can rest until dinner?''

Midnight. And she hadn't been able to sleep. Again.

Angel leaned against the kitchen counter, waiting for a cup of tea to heat in the microwave. She'd hoped it might be different if she felt safe. Here, there would be no telephone calls with silence on the other end. Here, there would be no anonymous letters with carefully typed threats. Even her agent didn't know where she was.

Her agent—holy smokes! Angel struck her forehead with the palm of her hand. She couldn't believe she'd forgotten about Karl. She'd have to call him first thing in the morning.

She lifted the cup of herbal tea out of the microwave and wandered into the large, informal living room, shutting off the kitchen light and switching on a single small lamp as she went. The room was decorated in soft earth tones that suited its Southwestern motif. Tea in hand, she was about to sink into one of the comfortable-looking recliners when a display of photos on the rough beams of the floor-to-ceiling shelves caught her eye. Curiosity aroused, she moved closer.

The photos covered three shelves. The first one she examined was a black and white of a very small girl riding astride a somewhat older boy, who knelt on the floor as if he were the child's pony. The children both had dark curly hair—the little girl's reached nearly to her waist and she looked as if she was giggling. Dulcie and Day.

There were several more of Dulcie, school pictures in which childhood's gamine charm clearly showed the promise of beauty. And there was an equal number of her brother. Day smiling and laughing, white teeth bared in a grin as he changed from boy to man. He looked so approachable. Was this really the same man she'd met earlier?

Slowly she moved on, examining the other pictures on the shelves. A second one was filled with even older photos. Kincaid parents and grandparents, stiff and unsmiling in formal photographs. The third shelf...

Baby pictures. Toddler pictures. Scene after scene of little Beth Ann as she grew from a tiny scrap of black-haired humanity into the sweet, shy tot Angel had seen today. Before she could sidestep it, the old hurt had reared up and grabbed her by the throat.

Emmie. She placed a hand across her mouth to prevent the sob that caught in her chest. If things had been different, she might have had a home like this, and these might be pictures of Emmie...her own precious child, who would be sleeping where she belonged, in her own little bed in her mother's house.

But things weren't different. She'd made a decision that she'd pay for every day for the rest of her life. Each time she remembered that her daughter belonged to another mother and father now, each time she remembered the wrenching agony of handing her two-month-old baby to

its adoptive parents, each time that Adrienne O'Brien sent
her the yearly report and photo that the private adoption
had included, each time she saw someone else's little girl,
she would pay for her poor judgment.

Unable to look at the pictures for another second, she
headed out of the living room. The darkness was absolute
once she turned off the lamp. In L.A., nothing, but nothing, was as dark as it was here in Luna County, where
people were outnumbered by cattle and a person had to
drive miles to see the lights of a town.

She felt her way back to the kitchen in the dark and
plunked her mug down on the counter. When the furni-
ture had assumed a shadowy outline, she began to move
back to her bedroom. But she wasn't able to stop the flood
of memories as easily as she'd turned off the light.

She hadn't allowed herself to look back after the awful
day when she'd given up her baby to a couple who could
give her more than she could. Blindly, almost without
forethought or care, she'd concentrated on the modeling
and drama courses in which she'd enrolled. She'd been so
focused on avoiding any time to think that she'd taken any
role offered, from that very first commercial spot until
she'd woken up one day to the realization that she was at
the top of her profession, with an Oscar nomination to her
credit and numerous glowing reviews.

What was she going to do if she followed through with
her decision to stop acting? She moved into the dark hallway and felt for the banister at the foot of the stairs. People would say she was crazy, and maybe she was, but her
desire for normalcy, privacy, for a life in which she was just
another face in the crowd, outweighed anything else. Everything, perhaps, except her need to keep busy. To keep
from thinking. Because if she had too much time on her
hands, regrets about Emmie would consume her—

A large solid object barreled squarely into her, nearly
bowling her over backward. She gasped and managed to

bite back the scream that nearly escaped. Reflexively, she clutched at the object to keep herself from falling. Soft fabric. Hard muscle. Her palm scraped across a stubbled cheek. A man. Fear instantly closed her throat.

"What the hell . . . ?"

Reason reasserted itself at the plainly bewildered tone in the masculine voice, a voice she recognized. *Get a grip, girl, you're safe here.*

A small light pierced the darkness as the man who'd bumped into her snapped on a tiny lamp standing on a table against the wall. Angel blinked in its sudden glow, assessing Day Kincaid as her eyes adjusted. She'd been too unnerved by his unexpected antipathy earlier to really look at the man. But in the lamplight she realized that he was . . . quite something to behold.

As she'd noted before, he was several inches taller than her model's height. His face was rugged, craggy *handsome* beneath a thatch of dark hair quirking out in defiant waves all over his head despite a severe cut that revealed his ears. Handsome in a hard, weathered way that the picture-perfect actors she worked with could never achieve. High cheekbones cast deep shadows over the dimples in his lean cheeks. His mouth was partially concealed by a thick mustache, but she could tell that he wasn't smiling. She was equally aware of his scent—a fresh masculine soap mingling with the unmistakable smell of healthy male vigor.

"What are you doing running around the house in the middle of the night?" His voice was deep and gruff and not particularly friendly.

She braced herself mentally. "I couldn't sleep. I made myself a cup of tea." She was annoyed at the timorous quality of her voice, but darn it, he'd scared her. Belatedly she realized she was still holding his forearm. She let go and stepped back a pace, straightening her robe.

Silver eyes the color of new coins watched her fingers pull together the gaping edges of her robe, then trailed down over the rest of her body before leisurely coming back to her face. She hadn't noticed the unusual color of his eyes earlier today. They were striking eyes on a man or a woman. On this man... She became aware that they were inspecting her with a thoroughness that made her very conscious of her own lack of attire.

Angel held the silky fabric closed with one hand and summoned her poise. "If you'll excuse me, Mr. Kincaid..."

"No." He didn't move.

She lifted her head, fixing him with a haughty stare, one eyebrow raised. "I beg your pardon?"

"I'm sorry if I hurt you today," he said.

His tone was so grudging that she nearly laughed aloud as her momentary sense of alarm passed. "Dulcie made you promise to apologize," she guessed, and was rewarded when he shifted his gaze to the floor.

"I really am sorry," he repeated. "I'm not in the habit of treating strangers, especially women, like that, but I thought...it looked to me as if you were trying to kidnap Beth Ann."

"I understand your concern," she said. And she did. If she had thought someone was luring her child away, she'd have reacted in much the same manner.

"I doubt you do." His voice was cool, yet she heard a thread of what sounded like desperation in it. "My ex-wife is Jada Barrington."

Jada Barrington! Even in Hollywood, the woman's reputation for excess and self-indulgence was legendary.

"I see you know her."

"I know *of* her," she stressed. "Believe me, we don't frequent the same circles."

He continued as if he hadn't heard her. "She didn't have the time or the patience to deal with an infant, but now she thinks I'm just going to hand over my child to her so she can play the role of devoted mother whenever she isn't too busy.''

The bitterness and anger came through clearly, and she began to see why he was so abrupt with her. Jada Barrington was an actress who worked in television. While her current series was excellent and she had a large following, she was widely known to be a difficult actress to work with as well as a wild woman in her time offscreen. Angel had made her name in movies but Day probably equated them as the same brand of trouble. Perhaps he even thought Jada had sent her!

"You don't—"

But he cut off her response. "I'm not telling you this to elicit sympathy. I'm telling you because now that you're here, you're as responsible as everyone else for Beth Ann's safety. If you see anyone who doesn't belong on this ranch at *any time,* you let me know immediately.''

So he didn't suspect her of being in league with his ex-wife. In fact, he hadn't mentioned her career at all. Which was just the way she wanted it. Dulcie must have given him his orders. She nodded. "I'll only be here for two weeks,'' she reminded him.

Then the concern that she'd felt since she'd seen the child's pinched white face after the scene in the yard came back. "You know, Mr. Kincaid, behaving as you did in front of Beth Ann this afternoon can't be good for her. You don't want to make her terrified of strangers. Surely there's some middle ground. Perhaps you could even stage some 'safe' experiences with strange people so that she doesn't grow up fearing every face in the crowd.''

Day's expression would have been amusing if she hadn't been the target of the ire apparent on his face. "If I need advice, I'll ask for it, Miss Vandervere. Right now I suggest that you return to your room and get some sleep. We rise early and work hard around here. If you're planning on spending any time with Dulcie, you'll have to do the same.''

Late in the morning, Day parked his big pickup truck in front of the drugstore in Deming. He'd already been by the feed store, the grocery and the vet's office on his round of errands. The faster he got back to the ranch, the happier he'd be. He wanted to ride out and check the fence in the northwest pasture before supper.

Supper. Last night, Dulcie's guest had been seated across the table from him, and later he'd bumped into her in the hallway—literally. He might not be thrilled about the idea of having a guest on the ranch, especially while he was so worried about the custody suit Jada kept threatening, but he had to admit that Angel Vandervere was easy on the eyes. And when she'd come up against him fully in the dark house, he'd had a momentary fantasy of getting to know those lush curves intimately. She wasn't really his type, but after seeing her, he wasn't sure he could say what his type might be these days.

She was tall, taller than he normally liked his women, and she was a blonde. When he'd grabbed her yesterday, he'd been expecting blue eyes, but hers were brown . . . big and soft and intelligent-looking. Funny that he didn't remember her at all. But he figured the timing had been wrong when she'd lived in Deming before. Dulcie had told him that Angel had moved there in the seventh grade. That would have been his first year of college, and he had to admit that on the rare occasions he'd been home, he'd been a lot more preoccupied with trying to get Corinne Cantler horizontal in his pick-up than he had been with checking on his younger sister and her giggly adolescent friends.

He shook his head, amused by the memory. Corinne was a waitress in a local restaurant now, and even though she'd been married to Buddy Alderson for nearly fifteen years, she still liked to flirt. In a better humor than he'd been since yesterday, when he'd seen a total stranger baiting his child with candy, he strode into the pharmacy and made his purchases. He had to wait for an antibiotic prescription that one of the hands needed for an infected cut on his finger. While he waited, he idly scanned the racks of magazines and newspapers near the front counter.

He always got a hoot out of the headlines in the tabloids. One rag proclaimed that a three-headed baby had been born to a couple in Pakistan. Another chronicled the life of a professional football player who was suspected of hiring an assassin to kill a fellow athlete. A third speculated on the whereabouts of some actress who had dropped out of the L.A. scene without a word. He glanced again at the grainy photo of the heavily made-up actress in a skin-tight black sequined gown that plunged far beyond decency, taken the night of the Academy Awards. Angelique Sumner had a truly incredible figure—

The salesclerk called to him that his prescription was ready, and he started to move away from the magazines. Then, drawn by some instinct that raised the hairs on the back of his neck in inevitable dread, he looked at the tabloid photo of the Sumner actress again.

Angelique...*Angel.* A sick feeling rose in the back of his throat as he realized that the world might not know where Angelique Sumner was, but he did. *He'd left her sitting in his kitchen reading to his daughter.* Through narrowed eyes, he compared the picture with his mental image of Angel. The woman he'd met hadn't been bent on improving her looks, and if he hadn't felt and seen her curves revealed beneath that clingy robe last night, he'd never have noticed her figure beneath the loose clothing she'd worn during the day. She'd had on no makeup that he'd noticed and her hair had been confined in a careless knot atop her head. Even so, he'd recognized a classic structure in the bones of her face and the fine, smooth skin. Yes, with makeup and that blond hair loose and curly, she would become the unforgettable beauty before him. Fury rose, a red mist that kept him standing in front of the magazines desperately trying to master his rage before he lashed out and destroyed anything within reach.

Dulcie. She *knew* how he felt about actresses! How could she have done this to him? If the press found out where their quarry was, his ranch would be splashed all over the country in one of these trashy papers, especially if his connection to Jada was recalled. The privacy he'd worked so hard to keep for Beth Ann would be gone in the time it took a mean bronc to throw a green rider. His teeth ground together and he grabbed the tabloid off the shelf, throwing it on the counter with the prescription. Suddenly he couldn't get back to the Red Arrow fast enough.

Two

Day entered the kitchen quietly, resisting the urge to slam the door with all his strength. He couldn't believe he'd had this...this actress in his house for two days without even knowing it. He slapped the paper down on the kitchen counter. "What the hell is the meaning of this?"

Dulcie, who was chopping lettuce at the sink, jumped visibly. "Don't do that when I'm holding a sharp knife," she complained. But as she turned and caught sight of his face, her expression changed from irritation to wariness. "The meaning of what?"

"This." Day stabbed a rigid forefinger at the article and accompanying photograph. He knew his anger was written all over his face but he didn't care. "You know how I feel about having my private life exposed to the public. You know how hard I've worked to be sure Beth Ann is shielded from—from this, and yet you deliberately invite a woman you know will bring nothing but notoriety to visit this ranch."

"Oh, excuse me." Angel—no, Angelique—hovered in the doorway. "I didn't mean to interrupt a family matter."

He felt his temperature boil a notch higher at her unfailing politeness. Didn't the woman ever have an honest moment of irritation or pique? With an acid courtesy of his own, he said, "Come right in, Miss Sumner."

She froze, and her face showed shock for an instant before she wiped it carefully blank as she took a hesitant step forward. In that instant, he was suddenly sure his suspicions were correct.

He didn't attempt to hide the hateful sneer in his voice as he said, "I wouldn't want you to miss this discussion, particularly since you've had a hand in deceiving me. How long did you think it would take me to figure out who you were?" He shoved his face close to hers, so furious that he was shaking. "How stupid do you think I am?"

As soon as the words left his mouth, he regretted them. Jada wouldn't have missed such an obvious opportunity for a stinging put-down. But Angelique Sumner ignored it.

"Dulcie didn't intend to deceive you," she said. Her words were quiet, but he could see her delicate jaw set in a surprisingly pugnacious line.

"Oh, no?" He tapped the paper furiously with an accusing finger. "What am I supposed to believe? That she just conveniently forgot to mention her houseguest was one of Hollywood's darlings?"

Dulcie made a sound of angry protest, but again it was Angel—Angelique—who spoke. "Like me, I imagine she didn't realize it needed any mention."

"Why the hell not?" He was so mad he was yelling.

"I thought you knew who I was!" Angel yelled back.

He was so surprised that the quiet woman who'd been floating around the ranch for the past few days could raise her voice that he was momentarily speechless. She even looked shocked at herself.

Taking a deep breath, she said more quietly, "Dulcie and I have been friends since high school, long before I started acting professionally. I assumed you knew who I was before I came here."

Dulcie stepped forward to stand shoulder to shoulder with her taller guest. "I honestly thought you knew, Day. It wasn't meant to be a secret."

He had the distinct impression the two women were uniting against him. When they put it that way, his anger seemed all out of proportion. Still, he wasn't willing to back down so easily. He said, "If you weren't trying to hide anything, then why doesn't the press know where you are?" Again he pointed to the headline.

Angel sighed. "I deliberately didn't tell anyone where I was going. I needed some space to think, to make some decisions I've been putting off. When Dulcie extended the invitation to come to the Red Arrow, I knew it was an opportunity I couldn't pass up. She's not related to me. There are no obvious connections. I was careful about leaving town and I've been making an effort to be inconspicuous—"

"You don't say," Day drawled, giving an exaggerated glance at her dolled-up image in the photo and then looking back at her.

She paused and gave him an uncertain smile, clearly not sure whether he was baiting her or not. Then she said quietly, "I realize that you must have some strong reservations about my presence here. If you like, I'll leave."

"No!" Dulcie glared at Day. "She's not hurting anyone. Angel couldn't hurt anyone." She crossed her arms defiantly. "If she leaves, I leave."

Day grimaced. Given a choice, he would have accepted Angelique Sumner's offer to remove herself from his ranch. But he needed Dulcie. Pilar, the ranch housekeeper of thirty years, had retired when she broke a hip two months ago. Since then, he'd had to hire and fire three housekeepers.

Finally, Dulcie had agreed to come and stay with Beth Ann until he could find yet another replacement. If Dulcie left, he couldn't keep Beth Ann with him.

He'd had the idea of sending her to a baby-sitter's house while he was out on the range some months ago, but when Jada found out, she'd used it to make him look like an unfit father. No, he had to keep Beth Ann here. Which meant he needed Dulcie. Which meant he was stuck with Angel whatever-she-was-going-to-be-called for the next two weeks.

"All right," he said. "You win." He wasn't certain which one of the women he was addressing. "But no more secrets."

"It wasn't a secret." Angel's voice was firm and vehement. "But after seeing how worked up you are, I'd have to say you're right. I wouldn't have told you because I'd have figured you'd have a paranoid hang-up with my career."

"And you'd be right." His words were flat and unapologetic. Turning, he snatched his hat from the peg where he'd hung it and slammed out of the kitchen. As he passed through it on his way to the barn, the only refuge he had away from the house, he gave the door of the utility room a satisfying bang.

Sunlight streaming across her face woke her, making her squint and throw an arm across her eyes. Morning. Slowly Angel swam out of the depths of sleep, hating the exhausted feeling that always dogged her these days. Why had she thought it might be different, better, here? She was lucky to fall asleep before dawn. Same old story. She couldn't sleep, and when she did, she couldn't get awake again. Catch-22.

The clock said 9:25. She sat up, forcing herself out of lethargy. This was her third full day on the ranch and she'd hoped to help Dulcie with her chores. Sleeping in like a slothful vacationer was not what she'd had in mind. Besides, it would only confirm all the bad things Day Kincaid was convinced she embodied. Darn grumpy man anyway.

Her stomach growled loudly—past time for breakfast. Quickly she made her bed and dressed, leaving her face bare of makeup and confining her hair in a wide barrette at the back of her head. As she opened her door, her stomach growled again. Kitchen. Food. She was used to eating at the crack of dawn. She went down the steps and headed for the kitchen.

Dulcie was making cookies. As she entered the room, the delicious smell assaulted her empty stomach with an almost physical pain.

"Hi, sleepyhead." Dulcie smiled from the counter where she was working. "I guess you want some breakfast."

"Yes, but I don't want you to wait on me," Angel said as she lifted a still-warm cookie from the tray cooling atop the range. "I'll help myself."

As she turned to remove a brimming pitcher of orange juice from the refrigerator, Beth Ann peeped around the corner of the counter, where she must have been playing at Dulcie's feet. Two fingers were tucked into her mouth and a worried frown wrinkled her small forehead. Striking silver eyes exactly like her father's peeped from beneath a fringe of black bang as she assessed the newcomer.

Angel was struck by the cautious quality of the child's surveillance. It was as if she was testing the atmosphere to see if it was safe to show herself. Angel had spent much of the day yesterday playing with the little girl, and she'd thought they had gotten past the shy stage. What could make a three-year-old so wary? She decided to pretend everything was normal. As far as she was concerned, it was.

"Hello there," she said. "Is it all right if I eat a cookie for breakfast?"

The little girl giggled, her small face losing its anxious look. "No. Cookies are for d'ssert. Cereal is for breakfast."

"Out of the mouths of babes," Dulcie intoned. "Around here, the men expect some kind of dessert with every meal. I feel like all I do is bake."

"Why don't you let me help? I love to bake." Angel sat down with a piece of toast and the cookie she'd pilfered. "And please tell me what else I can do. I've been lounging around here like a guest in a resort hotel for the past few days."

"You've been entertaining Beth Ann, which can be a job in itself." But Dulcie threw her an assessing look. "If that was just a polite offer, you'd better tell me now. I'm desperate enough to accept any help that comes my way." She shook her head and smiled. "I never fully appreciated everything the housekeeper did until she wasn't here to do it anymore."

"Well, then, let me help." Angel looked forward to immersing herself in old-fashioned chores. Maybe while she worked, she could take a good look inside herself and figure out exactly what she wanted to do with the rest of her life.

"I can help, too," Beth Ann announced. She gave Angel a mischievous smile. "Af'er you read me more stories."

"Oh ho! So you like my stories, do you?" Angel patted her knee and Beth Ann immediately scampered across the floor to climb into her lap, wriggling like an enthusiastic puppy. "So what stories shall we read today?"

Later, she finished mixing the filling for the crème de menthe brownies she'd made for dinner and set it in the refrigerator. As she swept the kitchen floor and ran a bucket of water to mop it, she thought again about her future. And her past. She'd once thought that money would solve all her problems. If only it could be that easy! Even before the anonymous stalker had begun his campaign of terror, she'd been thinking of leaving the world of scripts and cameras. Building the illusions that went into a film had been consuming enough to help her through the bad time after Emmie's adoption, but somehow it wasn't really her.

So who was she anyway? She sighed as she saw Day riding a big black horse toward the barn. He sat the horse with a fluid grace that spoke of years in the big Western-style saddles. Despite knowing what he thought of her, she found her gaze drawn to him again and again. Yes, he was handsome, but she was used to handsome men. She knew many of them were as shallow as their physical beauty.

Then why wasn't she able to ignore him? Any time he was in the vicinity, her antennae quivered and twitched with a fascination she was afraid could prove fatal if she didn't keep it under strict rein. For heaven's sake, the man didn't even like her! As she watched, he swept off his hat and beat it against his leg, sending a swirl of dry New Mexico dust off on the light breeze. His dark hair gleamed with fiery highlights under the merciless sun, and as one of the hands called out to him, she saw his white teeth flash in a grin.

He was vibrant and full of life, a complex man who wanted to rid his ranch of her presence as soon as possible. He saw her as a flat, one-dimensional creature. Actress. To him, there was no more to her than that. After hiding from herself and her feelings for so long, she was afraid his contempt might have some merit.

"Are you cooking, Miss Ban-ban-banderbeer? Can I stir?"

Shaken from her introspection, Angel looked down. Little Beth Ann stood beside her, poised to climb onto a nearby stool but obediently waiting for permission. Angel's heart softened in immediate pleasure.

"Of course you can help me, honey," Angel assured her, smiling as she lifted the child onto the stool, then hugged her close for a moment. Beth Ann was warm and pliable, wrapping her arms around Angel's neck and returning the hug.

"I'm a good stirrer," the tot told her solemnly.

Angel stifled a smile. "I bet you're the best. Did you just wake up from your nap?"

"Uh-huh. Aunt Dulcie said if I didn't get in your way, I could help you." The little face sobered, that entirely too-adult anxiety creeping into her tone. "I promise I'll be quiet."

Angel studied the child. Who could have sought to stifle this precious baby's enthusiasm and curiosity? Indignation rose within her and she said, "You don't have to be quiet and you most certainly can stay. In fact, I'm not sure I can frost these brownies without your help. What do you say?"

Sunshine brightened the room as the child's face lit up. "Okay!" she shouted.

Angel laughed. "Okay," she repeated.

"What's okay?" The voice belonged to Day.

She looked up, a trace of defiance rising within her. She would not let him squelch Beth Ann's pleasure in the chore. "Shouting is okay. So is helping me with these brownies."

"Oh." He eyed her and his daughter for a minute. "Thank you for letting me shout."

"Daaaddeee!" Beth Ann was giggling. "She meant me, not you."

"Are you sure?" He frowned as if he couldn't trust what he was hearing.

"Yes." The little one climbed down from her stool and bounced across the room to wrap chubby arms around

Day's knees. Then she climbed nimbly into his arms, shrieking with laughter when her father bussed her neck with his mustache. "I like Miss Banderbeer," Beth Ann announced. "Can she stay for a long, long time?"

Day hesitated. "She's only here for a vacation, filly."

"But why can't she—"

"Let's dance," he interrupted. Holding Beth Ann against him, he began to move around the room as the child squealed with glee.

Angel continued to frost the brownies, but she was all too aware of him. A quiet happiness filled her heart. Suspicions she hadn't been aware she harbored dissolved as she watched the way he responded to his daughter. Day clearly wasn't the one who had made her afraid to behave like a normal child. She hated to think ill of someone who wasn't able to defend herself, but it looked as if Day's dislike of his ex-wife might have some solid foundation.

She watched his long legs as he lifted Beth Ann and twirled once around the room in a three-step. His jeans were well worn and faithfully followed the muscled strength of his thighs. The child clung to his wide shoulders—

Her thoughts halted in disarray as the object of her thoughts met her gaze over the top of his daughter's head. Intent and thoughtful, his eyes held enough masculine interest to make her flush and return her own attention to her work.

When he moved his gaze from her, she could almost feel the change and she risked another quick glance at him. He was looking at his daughter again, smiling at the child. He set Beth Ann back on the stool beside Angel.

"Gotta go, filly," he said, brushing her cheek with his whiskered jaw until she squealed with laughter. "See you at dinner."

And he was gone. Just like that, the room drained of energy, vitality. In her mind's eye, Angel saw him dancing with Beth Ann, his large frame surefooted with a confident masculine grace other men could never hope to match. *Whoa, girl,* she told herself. *Don't get carried away. He's your host. Not your main squeeze.*

Day found Angel in the kitchen again after dinner, after he'd read to Beth Ann and tucked her in for the night.

"You sure are spending a lot of your vacation working," he said, setting a glass on the counter.

She smiled at him, up to her elbows in soapy water. "I don't mind," she said. "It's a welcome change."

That smile hit him right in the gut and he sucked in his breath. She was a beautiful woman. Too beautiful. He didn't trust the way she seemed to be infiltrating his life. "Don't get too used to it," Day warned, his voice harsh with hostility.

Her smile faded. So did the quiet happiness in her eyes. "We're not all the same, you know," she said.

"Who's 'we'?" He was wary, knowing what she meant without needing the answer.

"Actresses," she clarified. "We come in all shapes and sizes and colors, and our personalities are just as diverse."

If she'd gone any further, he'd have been able to get angry. As it was, her small rebuke did what feminine whining could never have achieved: it made him feel guilty. He hadn't been raised to treat people as he'd been treating her. Still...

"You're right," he said, seeking a truce without giving in. "I shouldn't judge all actresses by one lousy experience. But I find it hard to believe that you could be happy here, doing housework on a ranch when you're used to so much more. I keep thinking you must have some ulterior motive for wanting to help out. I'd like to know up-front what it is."

Her hands stilled in the dishwater and he knew he'd been right. She did have some hidden agenda.

"I need time—time to think," she said with a tentative look at him from under her lashes.

"Time to think?" he repeated.

"Yes. I have some . . . decisions to make that will affect my future, and I can't consider all the angles while I'm working. So yes, I guess I do have an ulterior motive." She picked up a pan, then pointed it at him for emphasis. "But that doesn't mean what I need has to be in conflict with what you need, does it?"

Put like that, she sounded so reasonable he could do nothing other than agree. "I guess not," he said. Then it struck him. They were having a conversation that consisted of something other than accusations and screaming demands. Given his suspicions, this whole talk could have degenerated into the very same kind of shouting match he and Jada often had.

If she were like Jada. She'd reminded him that she might be different, and in this respect he had to agree that she was. Intrigued by that thought, he pulled a kitchen chair toward him, straddling it backward.

"I'm curious. How did you get to Hollywood from Deming?"

She shrugged, shooting him a single startled glance while her hands hesitated in the water again. "The usual way, I suppose. I joined the drama club in high school and realized I liked acting. Other people told me I was good at it."

"And . . . ?"

"And so eventually I decided to try to make a living at it."

It was an answer but he wasn't satisfied. He studied her expressionless face, longing to shake her out of her habitual calm, wondering what piece of the puzzle that was Angel he was missing. Then he said, "You speak as if you didn't light out of town the day you got your diploma."

A half smile lit up her features. "I did. But I only went as far as Albuquerque."

Her eyes had a faraway look, seeing into some time and place from which he was excluded. It shouldn't have bothered him, but it did. "If you didn't go to Hollywood right away, what did you do?"

She came back then from wherever she'd gone. It was like watching someone in the distance gradually grow in size as they came nearer and nearer. Then she looked at him, and the pain in her wide brown eyes was a shock he wasn't prepared for. "I got married," she said.

He couldn't speak for a moment. If anyone came after him with a question, he couldn't formulate an answer if his life depended on it. All he could think was, *That wasn't in the magazines.*

She'd gotten married. He didn't like the feeling that simple sentence gave him, like an ugly, jealous fist that thumped into his stomach and stayed there like a lump of day-old oatmeal eaten in a hurry.

Finally sanity returned. And with it, the awareness that he hadn't responded to her bombshell in any way. He said the first thing that came to him. "Who to?"

The corner of her mouth kicked up a little, though it wasn't a mirthful response. "His name was Jimmy," she said. "He was from up near Albuquerque and I met him at a rodeo my senior year of high school."

Ah, he had it now. "And when the marriage didn't work out, you headed for Hollywood," he said.

"No." She emptied the last of the dishwater and hung the dishcloth up to dry, clearly signaling an end to his grilling. "I headed for Hollywood after Jimmy died."

Day wondered about Angel's husband all day as he rode his land checking each of the thirty-five wells that kept his cattle from dying of thirst in the arid desert region. She'd met him at a rodeo.... Had she married a professional

rider, one of the wandering men who followed the circuit
or had he simply been a spectator?

Had she loved him? Mourned his passing?

Cynicism reared its head as he recalled the information
printed in the article he'd read about her. One headline in
particular kept reverberating in his head.

A Legion of Lovers. The article had listed her numerous entanglements since she'd arrived on the West Coast,
detailing liaisons with famous men from every field of entertainment. He knew better than to believe it all, but sep-
arating the facts from the fiction was beyond him.

He made a last notation in the small notepad he carried
in his breast pocket, replaced it and wheeled his horse away
from the cottonwood well, so named because of the trees
that marked its location. Why was he still thinking about
Angel anyway? She was just a temporary guest in his
home.

And one of the most beautiful women he'd ever seen.
She had no business doing housework. He'd been too angry the first time he'd seen her to take in her appeal, but
since then . . . since then he'd found her difficult to ignore.
Though she didn't doll herself up like the woman who'd
posed for her publicity shots, he found her classic features
more striking each time he saw her. He'd already caught
himself fantasizing about pulling her hair out of the simple elastic band in which she habitually wore it and running his fingers through the silky, straight golden strands.
Yep, he'd caught himself more than once.

Fool, he told himself. *You've already paid the price for
one beautiful, useless woman in your life. When are you
going to learn?*

When he came in the door before dinner, she was in the
kitchen again, kneading dough with quick, competent
motions. Had she even been outside since she'd arrived?
Before he could give himself time to think, he blurted,

"Tomorrow, if you'd like, I'll give you a tour of the ranch." Then a thought struck him. "That is, if you ride."

"I ride, though it's been a while." She blew her bangs out of her eyes and turned the bread dough into a pan, covered it with a cotton cloth and reached for the next hunk of dough. Then she looked up from her work and smiled at him. "That would be lovely if it won't keep you from your work."

He shrugged, beaten to his knees by that smile. "I can do some work as we go."

He left her before he did anything more foolish than he already had, heading for his room to shower and change before dinner. When he returned, the men were starting to arrive, and Dulcie was carrying plates of food into the dining room. He walked into the kitchen, intending to help her carry dishes to the table.

Angel was perched on a stool at the built-in desk, the telephone cord wrapped around the fingers of one hand as she spoke into the receiver. Her face was alive with amusement and pleasure, more animated than he'd seen it since her arrival. He wondered who could put that look on her face.

Angel laughed as her agent scolded her for the tenth time. "Calm down, Karl. I'm fine. I simply needed a little space for a while. Just tell everyone that I'm taking a well-deserved vacation."

"Where on earth are you and why haven't you called?" Her agent didn't sound amused.

She guessed she couldn't blame him. It must be a bit nerve-racking to have your hottest property disappear without warning.

Karl went on. "I tried your number all day yesterday but all I got was that detestable machine you insist on using to screen your calls."

She forced a light laugh. Karl knew how much anxiety that screening diverted. Her anonymous caller had stopped trying to reach her after she'd installed that machine. Apparently he was too smart to leave a voice trail for the police. "What's so urgent it couldn't wait?"

Paper rustled over the wire and she could almost see him adjusting his glasses. "Well, Muffy Fenderson invited you to a—"

"Send my regrets."

"But Angelique, exposure is everything—"

"I'm not going, Karl. Anything else?"

He must have heard the note of finality in her voice. "Not really. Oh, some actor called, said he knew you and wanted your number to invite you to dinner. Janson Brand? I'd never heard of him."

She'd met him during her first days in L.A. Nice enough, but not an acquaintance she wanted to renew. All she did want right now was to be left alone. "Tell anyone who calls I'm unavailable for an indefinite period."

"Angelique!" Karl sounded almost panicky. "I can't say that. It will bring the press sniffing around with even greater fervor than they've already shown. Are you sure you're all right?"

"Karl, relax. I'm fine. You're the one who told me I needed a break, remember?"

"But, darling, I seem to recall I suggested the South of France, with me dancing attendance."

"The South of France sounds lovely. I'll consider it." She pressed on, conscious of a desire to conclude the conversation. Talking to Karl reminded her too much of all the things she wanted to forget about. "I'm going to be out of town for a few weeks. I'll call you when I get back, okay?"

"A few *weeks?*" Her normally unflappable agent sounded distinctly taken aback.

Angel laughed with real feeling. "Don't worry. I promise I'll call."

"No, wait! What if I get an offer you can't refuse? At least give me your number."

"All right." She gave him the Red Arrow number. "But don't call me unless there's an emergency. I'll call you when I'm ready to come back."

After dinner, she helped Dulcie clean up.

"I'll wash, you dry." Dulcie tossed her a dish towel. As she ran a basin full of water to begin soaking the pans, she said, "You've surprised me."

"I have? How?" Angel smiled as she put glasses into the dishwater, remembering that Dulcie used to be able to read her like an open book.

"You haven't asked a single question about how my brother got mixed up with a famous face like Jada Barrington."

"I did wonder—" Angel hesitated "—but I've learned the value of privacy and I try to extend it to other people." Then she grinned. "Besides, I can hardly imagine asking Day. Your brother isn't exactly thrilled with my presence here."

Dulcie sobered. "I know. And I blame every ounce of his attitude on Jada. Day has gotten a lot harder and a lot tougher since his marriage ended. The worst of it is, it's my fault they ever met. I regret that stupid bet every day."

"What bet?"

"The bet I made with Day." Dulcie sighed. "Several years ago we heard that Jada was filming a special project in Lake Valley, a ghost town north of here. They needed local cowboys as extras. I bet Day they wouldn't use him and he went just to prove me wrong. Jada took one look at him and decided that he would make great publicity. She was just starting out then, remember?"

Angel nodded. She thought of the way Day's jeans had molded his long legs, those unforgettable eyes and the easy confidence he wore like a favorite hat. It was easy to see how any woman would take a second look at Day Kincaid. But the man she'd met didn't seem the type to be easily manipulated by a woman. "So she bowled him over?"

"Not exactly." Dulcie's words confirmed her first thoughts. "But he was flattered by all the attention at first. Jada can be very persuasive, and for a while I think Day honestly thought she loved him. Anyway, I'll give you the short version. Jada got pregnant, and when Day found out, he married her even though he wasn't happy about it. She'd never have roped him otherwise. Jada thought Day would dance to her tune but when she found out he had no intention of ever joining her in L.A., they had some knock-down-and-drag-out fights like you can't imagine. The result was that she went back to L.A. before the baby was born. When Beth Ann arrived, Jada couldn't have been less interested. Day brought Bethie here when she was three days old, and until last year, Jada hadn't even seen her."

"What changed that?"

"Beth Ann is three now. As she got older, it occurred to Jada that the mother angle will enhance her somewhat soiled image. She's been insisting on visitation and hinting at custody for several months."

"That's awful if it's the only reason she wants Beth Ann." Doubt crept in because she couldn't imagine anyone not loving that sweet little girl. And she knew better than most how vicious the press could be. Maybe she'd been wrong in assuming that Jada had mistreated her child. Maybe the woman wasn't as bad as she had been made out to be. "Maybe she misses her and regrets the time she's lost."

Dulcie snorted. "And pigs fly. Whenever Beth Ann comes back from a visit to Jada, she's a silent mouse who's afraid of her own shadow. She's terrified of getting punished for getting dirty and she shies away from sudden movements as if she thinks she's going to get hit." Her face darkened. "Day's trying to get full custody and I, for one, am hoping he succeeds."

Angel thought of the love in Day's rough tones when he kissed his daughter's forehead, and of the way he'd given her his exclusive attention when he'd danced her around the kitchen earlier. There was no question that he adored his daughter. If what Dulcie believed was true, then she, too, hoped Day would succeed in gaining full custody, for the child's sake.

Three

When Day came into the kitchen before the crack of dawn the next morning, he was surprised to note that Dulcie must have gotten there before him. The lights and the radio were on and a cup of aromatic coffee, half-consumed, was sitting on the counter. A thud in the walk-in pantry alerted him to her whereabouts.

"Want me to start on lunches?" he called.

"Either that or the pancakes." Angel stepped out of the pantry, a loaf of bread and a dozen oranges carefully balanced in her arms. Her heavily lashed eyes were sleepy lidded and appealing; her bright hair spilled over one shoulder from the elastic band in which she'd confined it.

Too startled to keep silent, he blurted, "I wasn't expecting you!"

She gave a small shrug and smiled. "I told Dulcie to sleep in this morning, at least until Beth Ann gets awake."

Day pulled out one of the chairs and plopped down, pulling on his boots and stomping into them, surreptitiously studying Angel as she moved around his kitchen. She was dressed in jeans—not designer jeans, but sturdy work jeans faded from use—and a long-sleeved shirt that she'd tucked into the jeans. It was surprisingly serviceable clothing, even if it did fit her like a second skin, making him all too aware of the body beneath the clothing.

He thought about the offer he'd made yesterday in a temporary fit of insanity. A day in her company was going to be sheer torture. "You still interested in riding out with me this morning?"

"Yes." Across the room, his gaze met hers and she quickly dropped her own.

"You ever take your hair out of that ponytail?"

Startled, she looked up again. "What?"

"I said—"

"Yes. Sometimes." Her speech was rushed as if she was nervous. "But it's more practical to wear it this way, especially if I'm going to be working all day."

He digested that as he took the bread from her and started slapping thick ham sandwiches together. True, he'd offered to show her the ranch today, but he'd assumed that he'd swing back by the house about ten o'clock and prod her into action. He hadn't expected to spend the entire day with her trailing around behind him.

The telephone call he'd overheard last night replayed in his head against his will, and he wondered sourly if "Karl" was missing her more than she appeared to be missing him. The current lover, perhaps? One of several? She hadn't sounded sorry to be brushing him off as she had.

He watched her from beneath his lashes as she set the long table in the dining room with quick, efficient motions. She paused to heat the large cook pot and mix up a huge quantity of pancake batter, then threw on a large skillet of bacon and sausages.

"There are more of those brownies in the pantry from last night," she said as she filled a pitcher with orange juice and another with milk, then started a second pot of coffee.

He finished wrapping the sandwiches and brownies, assembling them into individual lunches with an orange and a bag of chips. Then he added a container of raw vegetable sticks and jugs of iced tea and water to each pile, as well, watching her expertly juggle the breakfast preparations.

One thing he had to say for her, she knew her way around a kitchen. "You do this kind of thing before?" he asked.

She paused to flip a pancake onto a waiting platter. "My daddy worked on a ranch up near the Black Mountains when we lived here before. I helped in the kitchen a lot." Her voice was husky and rich with reminiscence. "I know how much food it takes to feed hungry men."

He found himself reacting to the sound of her, the smell of her, clean, fresh and female, as she brushed by him to carry a loaded tray of food into the dining room. Scowling, he picked up another one and followed.

He didn't want to notice her. He didn't want to wonder if her breasts beneath the snap pockets of the traditional Western shirt were as round and full as they looked, if her slender hips and long legs would cradle a man as perfectly as he suspected. He didn't want to imagine what she'd look like sprawled beneath him with her hair flung over the pillow and her pouty lips begging him to take her.

But she was fast becoming all he could think about. *Only ten more days.* It was almost a prayer. *She'll be leaving in ten more days.*

"...look like you got out of bed on the wrong side, Boss."

He became aware that sometime during his fantasizing he'd taken his seat at the head of the table. The speaker was Joe-Bob, the youngest of the cowhands he employed and one of the only three who weren't married. Wes, his foreman and right-hand man, was grinning as if he knew exactly what Day had been thinking.

Day scowled at them both. "Listen up," he announced to the table at large. "Here's the schedule for today...."

By the time he had finished detailing assignments and answering general questions, the meal was over. The hands stampeded through the kitchen to snag their lunches and the day began.

Angel, who had been sitting quietly at his left throughout the meal, began to clear the table. When she stood, his hooded gaze slid down her body despite his best intentions. As it reached her waist, the buckle on her belt caught his eye.

Without thinking, he slipped a finger through a belt loop on her jeans when she started to move toward the kitchen. "Whoa, there. What's this?" He raised a disbelieving brow. The buckle on her belt was the unmistakable silver prize buckle awarded to junior rodeo champions for barrel racing.

Angel shrugged. "I used to fool around with rodeo competition when I was a teenager."

He snorted, suddenly aware of the hot press of her flesh against the backs of his fingers. "Lady, if you won this, you did a hell of a lot more than fool around." He removed his fingers and stepped away, feeling that he'd narrowly escaped being burned. Damn the woman! She had enough sex appeal for five.

In her company, he was starting to feel as frustrated as a stallion penned in the stall next to a mare in heat. Worse, actually, because there was no way he could allow himself to take what his body wanted from this woman. Abruptly he turned on his heel and left the kitchen. He needed some air.

Corky came snarling out from under the porch to growl at his ankles until Day pointed a stern finger at the dog. "One of these days I'm gonna get rid of you, you old faker.'' The dog appeared ferocious to strangers, but everyone on the ranch knew he was all bluster and no business.

While Angel finished cleaning up the kitchen, he saddled his horse and another for her—not the placid little mare he'd first had in mind, but a spirited gelding that would more easily keep up with the work he wanted to accomplish. Still, until he saw her swing easily into the saddle, he hadn't believed she could ride so well.

Jada had hated horses.

He deliberately put the thought out of his mind as they rode out of the yard. Today he wanted to check on the stock in several areas of his range. Tomorrow he'd ride out with some of the men and cull the ones that weren't healthy, get them ready for sale.

The morning went fast. Angel was as good a rider as that buckle she wore had indicated. If she was in any discomfort, she hadn't made a peep and she kept up with his pace easily, handling the gelding's early liveliness with aplomb until he settled down to work. She had borrowed a hat from Dulcie's old collection and, riding beside her, he had the oddest feeling of... of rightness, as if he was meant to do this with a woman at his side one day.

Not this woman. He instantly rejected the idea. Angel lived a life-style foreign to his, one that he'd tasted and found as poisonous as the deceptively lovely tansy that covered his land in the spring.

The hours slipped away and the angle of the sun told him it would soon be lunchtime. He hadn't made lunches for Angel and himself because he'd planned a loop that would take them back to the house by noon. He liked to try to get in to the house to have lunch with Beth Ann a couple of days each week, except during branding, when there was no time for anything except the endless cycle of bawling calves and their anxious mamas. Circling around now to come back toward the house, he paused near the front entrance to the ranch road, where the rock columns with the Red Arrow Ranch sign suspended above them in black iron greeted visitors.

"See that bull over yonder?" he asked when Angel reined her horse in beside him.

She nodded. "The one with the white blaze down his forehead?"

"Yep. Don't forget that blaze. Old Red's the only bull on the ranch with that face. He's got a mean streak a mile wide, and it's directed solely at two-legged creatures."

Angel regarded the bull solemnly. "Why do you keep him?"

"He's a great stud. Comes from solid stock and his calves fetch good prices. And if we handle him from horseback, he's as docile as any bull is ever going to be." Day squinted into the sun. "I doubt you'll ever have cause to remember this, but I'll tell you anyway. As long as you're in a vehicle or on horseback, you're just part of the scenery to him. But don't ever let him see you walking around. Couple of years ago, he rolled a pickup over on one of the hands who had gotten out to check a bad tire."

Angel sucked in a breath and her face paled. "Did he kill him?"

Day shook his head. "Guy got lucky, dived back through the window and stayed inside even after Old Red turned it over." He laughed grimly. "We had to tranquilize the crazy animal until we could get the pickup towed."

Angel shuddered. "I'll remember."

Her voice was thready and he glanced at her in concern. "Hey, you don't have to worry. Like I said, as long as you don't walk around in front of him, you'll be fine."

"You went away to college, didn't you?"

Day raised his brow at the seemingly irrelevant topic. "Yes. I majored in agricultural economics at New Mexico State."

"That's why you don't remember me, because I moved here the year you left. But what you also don't know is that two years later my dad was killed in a bull-riding exhibition."

An icy shock ran down his spine. He vaguely remembered his own father telling him about a hand from the Double Dos who'd gotten hammered by a bull at a rodeo. "Did you see it?"

She shook her head, and he noticed that she seemed to be regaining her composure. "I was preparing for my own contest. When we heard that somebody had gotten gored, we all went running over to see—and it was my dad."

Day reached across the space that separated their horses and covered her hand where it lay on the horn of her big Western saddle. "I can't imagine. That must have been pretty horrible for a young girl."

"It was." She looked at him, her eyes unusually sober, and he realized abruptly how gently good-humored she was most of the time. A man could get used to that kind of quiet presence at his side. If he was the kind of man who needed that, which he wasn't, he reminded himself.

The ride back to the ranch house from the road was only a few miles, and they rode into the barn in plenty of time for lunch. The last half hour, he was aware of Angel trying to find a more comfortable spot in her saddle.

"Ooh-ouch," she said, shifting in her seat as he dismounted. "I enjoyed that so much I forgot I'm not used to hours of riding anymore. I'm going to be sorry later."

Day held up his arms. "C'mon, softy, I'll help you down from there."

She smiled ruefully, grimacing as she slid out of the saddle, but the expression faded as his hands clasped her waist and drew her down before him.

He set her on the ground. He knew he should remove his hands from her soft flesh, step back and break the moment, but all the willpower in the world couldn't have made him release her. Her gaze clung to his, her eyes dark and inviting, and all around them the smell of leather, horseflesh and hay warred with the peculiar feminine fragrance that his body already recognized as being uniquely hers. Damn, but she'd gotten under his skin fast. Unbidden, the thought came that she'd probably done the same thing to hundreds of other suckers.

How many other men had been seduced by those eyes? How many others had inhaled that scent, or been driven crazy by the subtle, soft invitation of her body so near?

It was an intrusion, an uncontrollable break in his concentration, and he recoiled as if she were a rattler delivering a warning buzz. The telephone conversation he'd overheard came back to him and he told himself not to be a fool. This woman had legions of men at her feet already. He wasn't going to be one of them.

"Who's Karl?" he asked aloud.

Her forehead wrinkled and the clouded bemusement in her eyes gradually cleared. "Karl? He's my—" She stopped and her brows snapped together as the accusation in his voice registered. "What business is it of yours?" she demanded in as sharp a tone as he'd ever heard her use.

Day turned away, unwilling to acknowledge the jealousy eating at him, and began to unsaddle his horse. "Anything that happens on my ranch is my business," he said in a deceptively mild tone. "If your lovers are going to start showing up after you dump them, I want to be prepared."

"My—?" She stepped back a pace and shook her head as if to clear it. "What does Karl have to do with— You think Karl is my lover?" Her voice rose at the end as if she found the very idea unfathomable.

Hell, for all he knew, maybe the guy was her husband. He forced himself to tune out the snippets of intimate conversation he'd overheard and concentrated on unbuckling her saddle and heaving it off her horse, but she slapped his hands away.

"Just go away. I can take care of my mount myself." She was madder than he'd ever seen her, red flags of color staining her fair cheeks, her brown eyes nearly black.

"I don't think so," he said. "This animal is my responsibility, and I'll stay until he's properly cared for."

She practically gritted her teeth at that and he could see her mouth working in impotent rage. She led the horse to his stall, but in the middle of brushing him down, she whirled with the brush in her hand, pointing it at him like a weapon.

"Karl is my agent," she said in a voice that shook with fury. "And if you have any other sleazy thoughts floating around in your head, you can keep them to yourself because I'm done worrying about what a jerk like you thinks of me!" She put the horse away, gave him feed and fresh water, cleaned her tack in icy silence and then turned on her heel. "Thank you for the tour," she said with icy politeness as she stomped out of the barn.

Behind her, Day couldn't suppress a grin. She sure got high-and-mighty when she got mad. And Karl was her agent, not her lover. But the grin faded as he remembered the headline on the tabloid he'd picked up the day before. She might act offended, but nobody could collect a reputation like that without there being some grounds for it. His ex-wife was living proof of that.

For the next several hours, Angel pitched in with all the housework she could, which suited her fine. The clean air, the simple yet necessary tasks, the solitude... all were working their magic on her taut nerves, even if Dulcie's pigheaded brother was determined to believe the worst of her. Determined not to let him get to her, she hummed to herself as she pegged the last of a basket of sheets to the clothesline, then retraced her steps into the house. Passing through the utility room, she entered the laundry room at its opposite end.

It was amazing how many sets of clothes a big man working outdoors could dirty. She grimaced as she started the washer for a load of shirts, then bent to remove several pairs of long-legged jeans from the dryer as the washer chugged into another cycle.

Day's, she thought. She knew the three hands who lived in the bunkhouse took care of their own laundry and the other three were married, so these clothes must belong to Day. Day... he fascinated her against her will. Something about him appealed to her senses, called to her so strongly that she had to fight back the urge to seek him out, to resist trying to get to know him better, even though he'd been less than welcoming. It would never work anyway. He couldn't stand her.

But down deep, she thought he must be a good man. In the days she'd been here, she'd seen how hard he worked. And yet he always had time for Beth Ann in the evenings, no matter how exhausted he appeared. The kind of man she'd dreamed of meeting someday.

The kind of man that doesn't exist, she reminded herself.

Her next handful of fabric yielded a tiny pair of overalls, and she smiled, her mood lightening. She was going to have to keep in touch with Beth Ann after she left the ranch. The thought was incredibly depressing. In just four short days, the little girl had woven herself into Angel's heartstrings in a way Angel knew was going to last forever. As Beth Ann grew more used to Angel, she was beginning to chatter uninhibitedly, following her around the house to "help" with the chores Angel volunteered to do. The only reason Beth Ann wasn't with her right now was because she'd gone down for her customary nap after wheedling Angel to read her two stories.

Angel smiled to herself as she lifted the basket of clean clothes and started back through the utility room toward the kitchen. Beth Ann would be waking soon and she'd promised the little girl she could help make some custard for supper.

Two steps into the room she halted in confusion as Day slowly swung to face her from the sink where he'd been washing up. He'd removed his shirt and the vast expanse of his bare, tightly muscled chest met her stunned gaze.

The room, already small because of the two big freezers that took up space, seemed to shrink even more in size. She should speak. Offer a casual greeting. But somehow she couldn't quite remember how to utter the words.

His shirt was wadded in a muddy ball in the sink and the jeans he still wore were caked with mud down one leg. His chest gleamed where the water he'd splashed on his face had dripped down to caress taut pectorals. As he reached into the sink and held up the shirt he'd been rinsing, muscle bunched and rippled, drawing her attention to the sculpted planes of flesh. His chest was nearly hairless except for a T-shaped dusting of hair that spread across his breastbone and arrowed down the midline of his body. Flat copper nipples the size of quarters peeped through the hair across his breast.

"I got into a mud-wrestling match with a heifer," Day said.

Her gaze flew to his, and she felt her cheeks color at the amusement in his eyes. He knew she'd been standing there drooling over him!

"Oh. Who won?" It wasn't a brilliant comeback but at least she'd managed a sound. She was aware that he was assessing her—probably trying to decide if she was still angry, she thought.

"I'm still trying to figure that out. She looks about like I do right now."

She seriously doubted that, trying to ignore what seemed like acres of male flesh exposed to her view. With an effort, she unstuck her tongue from the roof of her mouth and concentrated on his words, hoping for a businesslike tone. "I just put a load of shirts into the wash. Why don't I throw that one in, too?"

Day hesitated. The amusement had faded from his eyes and he seemed to be searching for words. "Angel—Angelique—hell, I don't even know what to call you!"

"Angel will do," she said coolly. It was clear that he wasn't going to forget who she was. Or who he *thought* she was.

"I'm sorry if I jumped to conclusions about your phone call," he said with stiff courtesy.

She shrugged. "Consider it forgotten." She couldn't take her gaze from his mouth. The way his lips formed his words beneath the dark mustache was hypnotic. She didn't want to fight with this man. Before she could regret it, she blurted out, "Why did you think Karl was my lover?"

His eyes grew cool, hardening to chips of diamond. "You forget I've had experience with your type before."

"I don't consider myself a 'type,'" she said. "You're a person whose profession is ranching. Are you exactly the same as the rancher on the next spread over?"

"No," he said cautiously. "But you have to admit the life-style that goes along with your profession—"

"Affects individual personalities in individual ways," she finished. "Did Dulcie tell you why I'm here?"

He looked blank. "To vacation, visit her." He glanced pointedly at the basket of laundry she carried. "Although I have to admit your idea of a vacation differs from mine."

She refused to be charmed by him when he insulted her with every other sentence. "I'm thinking about getting out of movies, and I needed some time away to think about all the angles."

"What would you do? Television? Live theater?"

She shook her head. "No, I mean a complete withdrawal from public life. I just want to be a normal person."

His face registered nothing but skepticism. "Wouldn't it be tough to give up all the adulation?"

"Not at all."

"Ha. My ex-wife wouldn't be able to survive without her name in the headlines at least once a week."

"I'm not your ex-wife," Angel muttered through her teeth.

The telephone rang, interrupting her words. Day stretched an arm to the phone on the wall beside the back door. "Red Arrow Ranch, Kincaid speaking."

Angel hefted the basket of laundry to carry it upstairs. This was as good a time as any to make her escape. It was apparent that Day wasn't going to change his opinion of her. All she was doing was wasting her breath trying to reason with him.

As she turned toward the door, she heard him say, "I'm tired of your threats, Jada. Beth Ann is not coming to L.A. again. Ever. And another thing. Your calls aren't welcome here. If you have something to say to me, say it through your lawyer."

Jada! Dulcie hadn't been kidding about his ex-wife trying to take Beth Ann. As she carried the clothing upstairs, she decided that while Day's attitude toward her was inexcusable, he probably equated anything that smacked of Hollywood with Jada Barrington right now.

The thought depressed her out of all proportion.

Four

Day heaved a sigh as he sat in his office that evening. Dinner had been a charade with Angel avoiding even the most fleeting eye contract with him and Dulcie watching the two of them and then treating him to her dirtiest stare.

He felt like a fool. Angel had been right. He had no excuse for the unfounded accusations about her extracurricular life earlier in the day. Wearily he scrubbed both hands over his face. He felt old...cynical. Marrying Jada had changed him in so many ways. Sometimes he hardly recognized himself anymore. It wasn't pleasant to think that one bad apple had soured him on fruit forever.

He was going to have to try harder not to let his antipathy toward entertainers extend to Angel. She was a guest, a friend of Dulcie's. He couldn't remember Dulcie ever inviting a friend to the ranch before, so he knew the two women must be close.

Surely he could treat her with civility for the next few days. He knew he'd been touchier than usual since the day

Angel had arrived on the Red Arrow. With that fall of sunshiny hair, those wide spaniel eyes and that incredibly sexy, loose-limbed way she had of getting herself from place to place without seeming to exert any effort... He sighed again, testing the strength of the pencil between his fingers. He just needed a woman. That was all.

For a long time after Jada, he hadn't wanted to go near a woman. Finally, last year, he'd met a widow in Las Cruces who had needed her itch scratched in much the same way he had. The no-strings arrangement suited them both. He'd meant to call her after this last trip to L.A. but somehow the appeal was gone.

If he was honest with himself, he knew why, too. He'd spent the past several days fantasizing about long, slender legs wrapped around his waist and long blond tresses spread out across his pillow. She didn't do a thing to pretty herself up, but when a woman started with the kind of raw material that Angel had—

The pencil snapped.

Day swore. He looked ruefully at the two halves of the broken pencil. Hell. She was going to be here for less than two weeks. Surely he could control himself that long. And then she'd go and his life could get back to normal again.

He tossed the pencil into the trash and selected a new one, then tried to focus his attention on the breeding program displayed on the monitor before him. Breeding...mating. His common sense told him to stay away from Angelique Sumner, but the mere thought of mating with her was enough to make his body react predictably.

Yep, no question but that she'd thrown his mind into a total spin. And it wasn't just her sex appeal, either.

Having a strange woman around the ranch reminded him all too vividly of the days of his short-lived and disastrous marriage, even though Dulcie's friend couldn't be less like his small, curvaceous, man-eating ex-wife. No, she was nothing like Jada with her practiced, polished sexuality. He almost wished she was. Then he'd be immune.

Bile rose in his throat as he thought of Jada's last round of threats. She couldn't possibly take Beth Ann from him. Could she? No judge in his right mind would award custody of a small child to a woman whose loose thighs were a legend, even in Hollywood. But what if the judge was a woman?

Thank God he had his baby back. Wasn't possession supposed to be nine-tenths of the law? And thank God he'd realized what damage Jada was doing to Beth Ann before she did any more than she already had. Every night, he prayed that, given time, Beth Ann would outgrow the fears that her mother's rough treatment and neglect had fostered.

It would take patience—

A child's cry echoed through the house. Beth Ann! She'd had nightmares off and on for months since the first time he'd let her visit her mother. As he sprinted for the stairs, Day cursed himself for not heeding those early warning signs.

He took the steps three at a time, skidding to a halt outside Beth Ann's door to calm himself. He couldn't help her if she sensed how uptight he was. And then he heard a woman's voice, realized that the quietly reassuring murmur came from his daughter's room. He stepped into the doorway to see better.

In the dim glow shed by Beth Ann's night-light, he could see Angel seated on the side of his daughter's bed. Beth Ann was in her arms and she was rocking the child gently back and forth. "What's wrong, honey? Angel will take care of you."

Beth Ann whimpered, and his heart clenched painfully as she said, "I dreamed Mommy put me in a dark place and I couldn't get out. I was hungry."

Even in the dark he sensed Angel's recoil at the implication of those whispered words. She gathered Beth Ann closer, continuing to rock as she said, "No one's going to put you in a dark place, Beth Ann. I'm going to stay right here with you until you fall asleep again and your light will stay on all night. See?" She pointed at the sizable nightlight Day had bought after Beth Ann's first visit to her mother.

His daughter seemed content with that, and she snuggled deeper into Angel's arms with one small thumb in her mouth, the other hand firmly clutching her beloved blanket. As he watched, Angel lifted her face to the ceiling, and he was stunned to see the glitter of tears on her cheeks.

Moving into the room, he knelt beside her. "Hey, filly," he said to Beth Ann. "Daddy's here." And to Angel he said, "I'll take her."

Angel moved immediately to shift the child into his arms. As he slipped a palm beneath his daughter's little body, the back of his hand pressed firmly, for one fleeting instant against a mound of warm, soft female flesh covered by thin silk. His gaze flew to Angel's, but she was looking down at Beth Ann. Unable to stop himself, he took in the picture she made, the fall of hair he'd been dreaming of finally slithering around her shoulders and the short silk kimono she wore. Was she wearing anything beneath it? It sure as shootin' hadn't felt like she was. The robe overlapped across her breasts, but Beth Ann's snuggling had dislodged the fabric so that a deep valley of shadow beckoned. Farther down, long, smooth legs were exposed from midthigh to toe, and if he hadn't had his hands full, he would have been hard-pressed to keep from sliding an appreciative palm down that inviting length.

As he settled Beth Ann into his arms, a warm, dark scent assailed his nostrils. His body, already stirring with awareness, took a giant leap to life. Was this how his stallion felt when he scented a mare in heat? Hell, it was no wonder he acted so wild. Day felt pretty wild himself.

"Thanks," he said brusquely. "You can leave us now."

She went still. Then, without a word, she removed her hand from Beth Ann's clasp and rose. But as she started toward the door, Beth Ann stirred in his arms and began to whimper. "No! Angel, stay. Daddy, I want Angel." The whimper became a full-fledged wail.

Quickly Angel pivoted and stepped back to his side. "It's all right, Bethie. Your daddy's here now. He can stay with you."

Behind them, Dulcie stuck her head in the door. "Do you need me?"

"Beth Ann had a bad dream," he answered. "I'll handle it."

"Suit yourself." Dulcie disappeared and he heard her bedroom door close again.

Beth Ann had twisted in his arms and her tiny hand clutched at the short hem of Angel's robe. "Angel, stay here," she said, yawning.

He could see that she was falling back to sleep. Angel was still standing before him and he commanded her, "Sit down beside me until she's asleep."

She sat. She left a discreet space between them but the mattress dipped enough under their combined weight to send her sliding against him, her bare leg against the rough seam of his jeans.

Day gritted his teeth. Beth Ann still had the hem of Angel's robe in one hand and one flap was pulled up to expose a silken shadow of inner thigh. What would it be like to touch her there? To slide his finger between those thighs, up perhaps a scant inch until he was stroking the sweet woman's heat he knew was sheltered there?

Angel cleared her throat. "I think she's asleep."

Did he imagine it or was she breathing too fast? He wanted her! He hadn't felt like this since—

Since he'd met Jada and been so hot for her he'd gotten her pregnant like a teenager without a lick of sense.

The thought was like a dip in the horse trough on a chilly morning. Immediately every vestige of desire vanished. "Get out of my way," he growled.

Angel sprang off the bed as if she'd been burned. Beth Ann's little hand had gone limp in sleep and Angel's robe flapped around her thighs as she vanished from the room.

Carefully he laid his child in her bed and covered her, taking a moment to caress one satiny cheek. If anyone—any woman—thought she could take this precious gift away from him, she would damn well have to think again. He bent to kiss Beth Ann's forehead but his mind was already on the battle he sought. Two steps to the door and four more down the hallway. A light showed from under the door and he didn't bother to knock.

The knob turned easily under his hand; he was in the room before she even saw him. Angel spun at his entrance. She'd loosened the robe and appeared to be about to shed it and climb back into bed. With a stifled gasp, she shrugged the robe back over shoulders that gleamed a creamy pearl in the light from her bedside lamp. A part of his mind appreciated the glimpse of smooth pale flesh that had been exposed through the robe's opening when she whirled.

But he was too angry to dwell on it. "What the hell do you think you're doing?" he demanded, closing the space between them until he was only inches from her stunned face.

Angel was still for a moment, much as she'd been earlier, and he realized she was marshaling her defenses, not quailing in fear as he'd half hoped.

"I was getting ready for bed," she said coolly, quietly. "Until you barged in here like a madman." She deliberately raised a hand and inspected beautifully shaped fingernails, then lifted her gaze to his. "If you think I'm going to apologize for comforting a frightened child, you can think again."

Her eyes held nothing. Her face had gone blank and still, totally unreadable, and he saw that she was blocking him out. The knowledge made him even angrier. "Comforting a frightened child? Is that what you call it?" he sneered, pushing his face even closer. "Listen, lady, I don't need your help raising my daughter and I'll thank you to stay away from her. I won't have you manipulating her emotions so you can get close to me. Her own mother did enough damage for a lifetime. I'd just as soon you didn't add to it."

He'd gotten under her skin, he saw with satisfaction.

Her mouth opened once and closed again. "You think I'm—I'm being friendly to Beth Ann so I can get close to you?" Her tone took on a mocking note and her eyebrows rose in disbelief as her chin shot up several notches.

He was too wound up to heed the warning signals. "I think it's a distinct possibility. And I'm warning you to back off. I have no intention of letting another woman into my life, so if you're playing up to Beth Ann in hopes of hooking me you can forget it."

"*Hooking* you?" She practically spat the words at him. "Are you under treatment for these delusions? Any woman in the world would love that little girl, but once she found out she had to take you as part of the package, I can guarantee you she'd think twice." She tilted her chin up another degree. "How a surly grouch like you could have fathered such a darling child is beyond me! Just in case you're not getting the message, let me put it more clearly. The last thing on my mind is a liaison with you, Romeo."

He shifted from foot to foot, itching to plant a fist squarely against that haughty jawline, but a deeply ingrained protective instinct held him back. "Oh, yeah?"

She stared at him through narrowed eyes that practically shot flames. "Yeah. Not for a hundred bucks."

"No?"

"Not in a million years."

"You sure?"

"Positive. Not even if you were the last man on Earth."

"You know what I think?"

"I don't care what you think."

"I think you're protesting too much."

"I am not." She was still nose to nose with him, but suddenly he saw that he'd gotten through. Feminine awareness sprang to life in her eyes and uncertainty dropped that maddening chin a full inch.

"You are," he said as he placed his hands at her waist.

"Wait! I don't want this—"

"Yes, you do." And he lowered his mouth to hers.

Angel went rigid with shock. She put up her hands to push him away, but Day pulled her hard against him, flattening her hands between them as his mouth covered hers. Her heart raced; the knot of tension in her stomach dropped several inches to center squarely in her abdomen.

His mouth was as hard as his body, yet warm and persuasive as it molded her with strong intent. Her protest died unborn. One of his hands still gripped her waist; his fingers slowly spread so that his thumb rested on her hipbone. Each millimeter of skin it covered on the small journey felt as if it would be forever imprinted with his searing brand. The other arm was a hard bar behind her back, his palm flattening her against him in inescapable demand. There, too, she imagined that the print of his hand would show on her sensitized skin for the rest of her life.

She knew she should fight, should scream, should refuse to yield to this masculine domination. But her senses were far too preoccupied with registering the unique scents and tastes and smells that were Day Kincaid to give much thought to protesting. She could no more prevent her mouth from moving under his than she could prevent her hands from crawling up to clutch at his broad shoulders.

She hadn't seen this moment coming, but her body knew without question that this was right, this was good, this was what she'd waited for... forever. One tiny part of her brain tried to stir, to warn her that this was just a man and not one who thought her particularly trustworthy at that, but it was overridden by the sensual explosions that registered everywhere his body touched hers. This wasn't just a man—this was *The Man*. With a moan, she softened against him, returning the pressure of his lips.

Her yielding was instantly recognized and accepted. Day shifted his hand from her hip around to join its companion at her back, pulling her even closer. Her breasts were flattened against his chest and even through their clothes she could feel the heat his big body gave off. His belt buckle dug into her torso, and below... below there was no mistaking the powerful strength of aroused man that throbbed against her soft belly, a tensile shaft of burning heat against which she automatically pressed herself in response.

Her lips parted under the insistent demand of his. When his tongue slipped along her bottom lip, she shivered helplessly, opening her mouth in an invitation he was quick to accept. The mating of their tongues felt right, a sensation she'd craved without realizing it.

She moaned again.

Day gathered her closer, though she couldn't imagine it was possible. His hands gripped her waist as he kissed a steady path along the line of her jaw to her ear. When his hot mouth took her earlobe in a strong suckle, she jerked against him with an involuntary gasp. Before her body could do more than jolt again in his arms, he'd moved on, down the sensitive cord at the side of her neck, across her collarbone and farther.

Lost in a whirl of stimulation, Angel drifted, each new heightening of her excitement plucking a fine wire of need low in her belly. He moved one hand slowly, leisurely, from her back to her ribs, stroking upward with smooth, subtle motions that completely failed to alarm her until, with one sneaky finger hooked into the fabric of her robe and matching nightie, he pulled the material aside and bared her breast to the cool night air.

She gasped in alarm. How had she allowed this to go so far?

He misunderstood the sound. "Don't worry," he said to her, his stroking fingers seeking and finding the taut tip of her exposed breast. "We're going to be good together."

"Day, wait. I barely know you." Her voice quivered and broke in her agitation as she pulled his hand away.

He kissed her temple without releasing her. "You know everything you need to know and so do I. I know you're tall and we're going to fit together like two sections of the same fence when we—"

"No! I mean, this isn't the kind of thing I do as a rule." Panic began to rise as she pushed at his unyielding shoulders.

"Rules are made to be broken, just like horses. And you're just like a skittish, long-legged mare right now." His silvery eyes were heavy lidded, compelling as he gazed down at her. "I've always had a good touch with mares. I'll be gentle with you."

As he dropped his head and sought her lips again, Angel began to struggle. The sensual lethargy that had stolen over her shattered. "I am not a horse. And I don't want the benefit of your gentle touch." Her voice shook. "I don't doubt you've had plenty of practice, but I'm not interested in being one of a long string of Kincaid's ladies."

Day's hands froze as her furious words struck home. "Then what are you interested in? What did you think we were doing?" he asked against her lips. He released her and she was shocked by the change in his voice. While he hadn't raised the volume by even a fraction, the humor was gone and a flat, dangerous chill had taken its place. "This doesn't mean a thing to me. There's only one thing I want from you or any woman and this—" he pressed his palm ever so lightly against her still-bared breast "—is it."

The curt words sliced through her, drawing blood. Angel drew in a shaky breath, turning away blindly to fumble with the closings of her robe. What had occurred between them hadn't been just sex. She couldn't sort out just what it was, but her reactions to Day made what she thought she'd felt for Jimmy an insipid crush in comparison.

She could feel the strength of her own arousal still burning within her, but she knew that she couldn't make love with a man who only wanted her body, despite her own desire. Slowly she turned to face him again. "I can't," she said baldly.

His nostrils flared, and for a moment she thought he was going to pull her to him again. "You can't?" he echoed. His voice was incredulous; it cut the air between them like a whip. "It sure as hell didn't feel like you can't." His face twisted and hardened into a mask of dislike.

She felt herself flush. "I'm s—"

But he wasn't listening. "It felt more to me like you were so hot for it you'd have let me take you standing up if that's what I'd wanted."

Shame crawled over her. Having her behavior so crudely analyzed was hurtful, but even worse, it was true. Stifling a sob, she sank down onto the edge of the bed and dropped her face into her hands.

Day made a sound in his throat, almost a growl—of frustration or fury, she couldn't tell which—before turning on his heel and striding from the room.

As her door closed with a soft, but very final click behind him, Angel lifted her head and wiped the tears from her face with a shaking hand. For the rest of her time at the ranch, she had to stay far, far away from Day Kincaid. Not because she was afraid of him. No.

Day touched something deep inside her with his caresses, with his fighting love for his child, with his determination not to let anyone hurt him ever again. No other man had ever touched her like that, and deep in the wise, feminine core of her, she knew that no other man ever would. Day could hurt her badly if she wasn't very, very careful.

Day gave her a wide berth the next morning, noticing that Angel seemed no more eager than he to speak. In less than a week, his world had been turned upside down and, dammit, he resented it! All he could think of was Angel. Did she realize he'd been lying when he told her all he wanted was the sex? Maybe that had been true the first day he saw her, but there was too much about her he didn't understand. She was right—she wasn't like Jada. But that didn't mean she wasn't just as dangerous in a different way. He didn't want to want her. He just wanted her gone.

Stepping into the kitchen at lunchtime, he found her there with Dulcie and his daughter.

Beth Ann raced toward him for her usual exuberant greeting. "Daddy! Hi, Daddy!"

He laughed and knelt on the floor to hug her, but her foot caught on the edge of the braided rug at the sink as she rounded the corner, and before he could reach her, she fell flat.

Time slowed to a crawl as she skidded and pitched forward. He saw the surprise then instant fear in her eyes as she went down hard on her side, unable to get her hands out to catch herself at that angle. Her little head hit the floor with a hard knock, and he involuntarily winced.

Time sped up again after that, but he felt frozen in place. Beth Ann stirred and began to whimper; the sound quickly changed to a shriek of pain. Already on the floor, he began to crawl toward his baby, but Angel was there ahead of him. Sinking down without hesitation, she lifted the little girl, enfolding her tightly in her arms and rocking her from side to side. Under her breath she hummed a comforting croon.

Beth Ann continued to scream uncontrollably. The sound grated on his exposed nerve endings and he gritted his teeth, about to demand Angel hand over his child.

Just as he reached out for her, Angel said in a quiet but firm voice, "Beth Ann, you need to stop screaming now. You're scaring Daddy and Aunt Dulcie, and I can't tell what's wrong with you unless you calm down. Now I want you to take a big, big breath for me."

To his astonishment, his daughter quit hollering. Tears continued to roll down her chubby cheeks, but she took a deep breath, which Angel encouraged her to repeat twice more.

Then Angel said, "I bet that was scary, slipping on that rug."

"Yeah." Beth Ann's lower lip quivered and she put a hand to the side of her head. "I falled and hit my head. Right there."

"Awww, let me see." Angel carefully parted the child's hair and peered at the spot. "No blood. But you're going to have a big ol' bump there for a few days. We'll have to be careful when we comb your hair. Would a kiss help make it better?" Beth Ann solemnly nodded and Angel drew the little girl to her and pressed a gentle kiss against the injured spot. "There." She looked over Beth Ann's head at Day for the first time. "If Daddy kisses it and helps you to put some ice on it, it will be better real soon."

He wanted to wring her neck. What gave her the right to comfort his daughter? But Beth Ann was looking at him expectantly and all he could do was take her from Angel's arms and kiss her poor little head, then accept the ice pack Dulcie wrapped in a towel and handed him.

"Why don't we sit in the rocking chair together and read a story until lunchtime," he suggested.

Day read two stories before Dulcie called them to the table, and all during the story reading and the ensuing lunch his anger grew. Beth Ann was his kid and *he* could provide the comfort she needed.

By the time lunch was over and he'd put Beth Ann down for her afternoon nap, he was in the mood for a rip-roaring confrontation. Charging down the hall, he burst into the kitchen. "I want to talk to you," he growled.

Angel was with Dulcie, poring over a recipe at the kitchen table. Dulcie, apparently seeing the look on his face, slowly got to her feet. "I'll leave so you can talk, but I'm warning you, big brother, if you forget that Angel is a guest here I'm going to shred your fanny for chicken feed."

He was almost distracted enough to smile, but Dulcie didn't look amused. In fact, she looked as if she'd kick him in the teeth if he laughed. Throwing his hands up, he said, "All I want to do is talk to her."

"Good," Dulcie said. Casting a last dark look at him, she walked from the room.

Angel was still seated at the table. Day walked over to stand across from her, but now that he was here, he didn't know exactly where to begin. Before he could open his mouth, she forestalled him. "I'm sorry if I took over when Beth Ann fell," she said. "I didn't stop to think. All I wanted to do was comfort her."

"You shouldn't have picked her up," he said, knowing his tone was full of accusation. "The first rule in an accident is to determine the extent of the injuries before moving the victim."

"Determine the... For Pete's sake, the child *fell*," she said. "She banged her head, but anyone could see that she was okay. All she needed was a little cuddling and some magic first aid."

"It wasn't your job!" he shouted, goaded by her assumption that he didn't know what was best for his child.

"Well, it was yours and I didn't see you hurrying to the rescue," she flared right back. "And if you'd made as big a deal as this out of it, she'd still be crying!"

Before he could answer her, the telephone rang. Day was standing right next to it and he snatched it off the wall. "What?" he barked.

"Day?" It was his lawyer and the man sounded rather taken aback.

"Oh, hi, Charley. Didn't mean to snap at you." He glanced over at Angel. "I was having a little trouble with some of the wildlife here."

Angel's eyes rounded, then narrowed in return.

"I have bad news," Charley said, and Day felt a leaden weight settle in his gut. Whatever it was, he knew it couldn't be good if Charley was calling him in the middle of the day. Charley usually called after dinner because he knew Day's schedule was so unpredictable.

"What?"

"Your ex-wife's attorney has filed a petition for full custody."

"What?" The word exploded from him. Sure, she'd threatened it, but she'd threatened a lot of things in the past and she hadn't followed through with any of them. "She can't do that!"

"I'm afraid she can," Charley said, regret in his tone. "She says she believes the child needs a mother figure in her life."

"A mother figure." His tone was pure scorn. "The last person I'd ever allow to fill that role in Beth Ann's life is Jada." Then the reality of the situation hit him. "What can I do to prevent her from succeeding with this?"

Charley sighed across the wire. "You mentioned once that you suspect your wife of neglecting, possibly abusing your daughter. We could try to prove that."

"What would we have to do?" He was eager to grasp at any lifeline.

"You'd have to have the child evaluated, counseled, examined for any medical corroboration."

"No can do." He didn't even hesitate. Beth Ann's world wasn't secure enough to withstand those kinds of probing investigations. He refused to traumatize her any more than she already had been. "I couldn't put her through that, Charley. She's only three years old."

"I was afraid you'd say that." The lawyer left a heavy silence to hang on the line.

"So what else can we try? What are my chances of winning without that?" Surely there had to be some way to beat this ridiculous custody suit. They couldn't take his baby away, could they? Deep inside, a cold fear spread. Of course they could. Jada knew nothing was more important to him than Beth Ann. This was her revenge.

Charley cleared his throat. Charley always cleared his throat when he didn't have good news to report and Day steeled himself.

"I don't know what your chances of keeping the child are," the lawyer said. "You aren't married. Since the child doesn't have a stepmother, you're at an automatic disadvantage. Courts still tend to favor the mother in a majority of custody cases."

"Yes, but my sister, Dulcie, Beth Ann's aunt, is living here now," Day reminded Charley. "Wouldn't she count as a mother figure?"

"Hmm." It was a noncommittal sound, but Day detected a hint of wheels turning in Charley's shrewd brain. "You might have something there, if we can prove that she is a permanent part of the child's life."

Day conveniently ignored the fact that his sister was only here at his request for an extended visit, and that she had a husband and a life of her own in Albuquerque. "Of course we can," he said. "Dulcie is as permanent as they come."

Five

She knew that the polite thing to do would be to leave the room so that Day could conduct his conversation in private. But when she saw his expression darken and heard the exchange between him and the caller, she realized what was happening. Wild horses couldn't have dragged her away at that point.

Just as Day put down the receiver, Dulcie came back into the kitchen. She looked askance at Angel, who had put a hand to the base of her throat, and at Day, who was staring at one of the far walls in a daze.

"What's wrong?" she demanded. "Who was on the phone?"

Day didn't appear even to have heard her.

"I think it was his lawyer," Angel said. Her voice sounded high and faraway and she cleared her throat. "Jada Barrington wants full custody of Beth Ann."

Dulcie's eyes widened, then a blaze of fury lit them. "She's got to be kidding," she said flatly. "That woman couldn't nurture a houseplant, much less a little girl. She can't have her."

"I might not have a choice," Day said hoarsely. His eyes were dull and worried and Angel's heart ached for him. "She's suing for custody on the grounds that Beth Ann needs a mother figure in her life."

Dulcie's face paled and Angel was sure her own looked much the same.

"But that's unfair," Dulcie said. "You're obviously the better parent."

"We'll have to hope the judge agrees with you," Day said. As he turned away, the defeated set of his shoulders betrayed his concern.

Watching him leave, Angel wished it was within her power to give him the one thing that would make him happy—the assurance that his child would never be taken away from him. She'd learned to live with the knowledge that she'd *given* a child away. How much worse would it be to feel that the decision wasn't yours to make, that your child could be taken by a judge who had never even met you until you became one of his cases?

After dinner that evening, Day had to check on a windmill that one of the hands had reported wasn't working earlier in the day, so Angel offered to put Beth Ann to bed. When the last story had been read, she tucked the little girl in with a gentle kiss on her forehead. "Good night, sweetheart," she whispered.

Without warning, Beth Ann threw her small arms around Angel's neck. "I wish you could always stay here with me and Daddy," the little girl said. "I wish I had you for a mommy."

The honest longing in the child's tones brought tears to Angel's eyes and she hugged Beth Ann closer. "You already have a mother, honey. But I'd be happy to be your friend."

"My friend who never goes away?"

Oh, boy. She wasn't going to be allowed to get out of this the easy way. Taking a deep breath, she said, "Beth Ann, you know I'm just visiting. I have a job in another place that I'll have to go back to soon." A white lie, but for a good cause. The child couldn't be allowed to imagine Angel in the role of her absent mother. It would be a cruelty when she left, as she'd soon have to do. Still, she couldn't resist adding, "But I promise I'll write and try to visit you when I can."

The little girl loosened her clutch then and lay back on her pillow while Angel pulled the covers securely around her and draped her blanket within easy reach. Pressing one final kiss to the little one's forehead, Angel straightened and walked to the door.

As she stepped into the hall, a large, dark figure detached itself from the wall and straightened to full height. *Day.* It might be dark, but her pulse leaped to a faster cadence. She'd know him anywhere.

She hesitated, but when he made no move, she said, "Beth Ann is ready to say good-night to you."

"Is she?" The deep voice was low, in deference to the child only a few yards away, but it practically vibrated with hostility. "You mean a touching good-night scene with her stand-in mother wasn't enough?"

Angel gasped. "I told her I wasn't—"

"I heard what you told her." Day caught the hand she'd thrown out in appeal and used it to drag her closer. "Don't toy with my daughter's feelings just because it makes you feel good to be needed. Her real mother has done plenty of damage. Beth Ann might think you're the greatest thing to come along in her young life, but I know better."

She couldn't believe that after all she'd done, he could still assume her every move was selfishly motivated. Fury rose and she spat out the words in a furious whisper, her normal cautious courtesy forgotten. "You are the most suspicious, the most unbelievably paranoid human being

I have *ever* had the misfortune to meet. Why must you as-
cribe ulterior motives to every move I make? Have you
ever thought that maybe I simply like children, and Beth
Ann in particular?''

She fell silent, suddenly aware of the strong, inflexible
grip he had on her arm, of the heavy sound of their combined breathing in the still hallway, of the heat of his big
body mere inches away. He smelled of healthy male sweat,
musky horseflesh and hay, though the combination wasn't
offensive. She could almost hear the wheels turn in his
mind, leading him to condemn her without a trial or even
the chance to make a statement.

"Can you tell me—*honestly* tell me—that you don't
have any vested interest in my daughter?'' His voice was
softer now, without the rough anger of a moment ago, but
no less threatening.

Vested interest? Angel opened her mouth to assure him
that she didn't, but a memory of Emmie, her own precious infant, floated across her consciousness and halted
her words. Emmie...Beth Ann. Perhaps her motives
weren't as pure as she believed. Emmie was unattainable
now, gone forever to a family who could give her everything that Angel had believed she couldn't. But Beth Ann
was here. And she needed Angel, needed her in a way that
called out to every mothering instinct she had. Was it possible that Beth Ann was replacing Emmie in her heart?

Her shoulders sagged. She was barely aware of Day's
grip loosening, allowing her to slide free.

"Angel?'' he asked in a hushed voice from which all
anger had drained.

She shook her head blindly. "I—I can't'' was all she
could say as she sought the privacy of her room.

Morning couldn't come fast enough. She'd lain awake
through most of the long, dark night, wrestling with feelings she'd successfully avoided for the past several years.

Finally, out of the miasma of unproductive self-flagellation and sorrow, she'd realized again that she couldn't change the past. All she could do now was look to the future and try not to be swallowed whole by regret.

The future... It stretched bleak and empty before her, a long vista of years dodging the press, trying to fade into anonymity. When she left the ranch, she was going to have to choose a new direction. Maybe during the next few days something would appeal. Ah, what was the point in thinking about it? She might as well head downstairs and help Dulcie, keep herself busy so she couldn't think.

After lunch, she tiptoed down with her boots in her hand so as not to wake Beth Ann. She hadn't had time to ride again since the first time Day had shown her the ranch, and she hoped to get out of the house for a little while. Beth Ann was napping after the story time they had begun to share every afternoon; the little one's eyes had closed before the end of the second book.

She paused inside the back door to stomp into her boots, then stepped outside into the sweltering Southwestern heat. Corky came out from under his bush long enough to offer her the obligatory snarl, then retreated. As she approached the barn, raised voices caught her attention.

"I'm not yelling *at you*. I'm just yelling! What the hell am I going to do now?" The voice was Day's.

"I don't know." Dulcie was the other speaker, and she sounded miserable and upset. "Day, I wish I could stay, but Lyle wants me home. This is my *marriage* on the line here."

"All right, Dulce. It's not your fault, I know. I didn't mean to shout."

This was clearly a private family matter. Angel started to tiptoe away, hoping that they would never know she'd been there. It wasn't as if she'd intended to eavesdrop. Although, to be honest, she was dying to know what the problem was be—

"Who's there?" It was a command, not a question, as Day appeared in the doorway of the tack room.

"I was just leaving." Angel realized her shadow had crossed the patch of sunlight that streamed into the room. Prudently she kept moving.

"Wait." He beckoned her into the barn. "You need to hear this, too."

"Hi." Dulcie sat on a hay bale, her face as shadowed as the interior of the barn. "I just got a call from Lyle. He wants me to come home right away."

"Oh." Angel sat down beside her, conscious of equal parts disappointment and concern warring within her. There was nothing she could do but make this easier for Dulcie.

"I'll get my stuff packed, and we can drive to Albuquerque together. I can arrange a flight from there."

"But..." Dulcie looked even more stricken. "I didn't mean that you had to leave, as well." She twisted to face her brother. "Can't Angel stay here until the end of next week? I'd hate to spoil her vacation."

Day had been leaning against one of the stalls. At Dulcie's words, his mouth flattened into an even thinner line and he straightened, planting his feet wide apart. He transferred his gaze slowly from his sister to Angel. As the silence stretched, she could read the refusal in his face. "Are you willing to continue helping out?" he asked.

"I...certainly." What was he getting at? And did it matter, if it meant she didn't have to go back to L.A. or anywhere else she might be found?

"I need somebody to help with Beth Ann and the house until I can find another housekeeper," he reminded her. "I'll put an ad in the paper this week, so if you're willing to fill in, you can stay until I hire someone."

She didn't have to ponder. The relief that swept over her was almost overwhelming. "I'd be happy to help."

"Great," said Dulcie. "I'll feel much better about leaving Beth Ann with you," she said to Angel.

"You don't have to leave her with anyone," Day said to his sister, and Angel wondered at the gruff tone of his voice. "You know you always have a home here."

"Thank you." She stood and kissed his cheek, and Angel was struck by the similarity in the two dark heads pressed close together.

As she rode out of the barn a few minutes later, she deliberately set herself to savor every moment of the experience. From the look on Day's face, he'd hated having to ask for her help, and she doubted it would be long before he'd found someone to care for the house and Beth Ann. This might be her last chance to enjoy a quiet ride in total solitude before she had to leave.

Leave the ranch... She forced back the panic that the thought created. Where could she go? She supposed she could quietly rent a place somewhere and hide out. If she was careful—and lucky—the press wouldn't find her.

But what would that accomplish? She couldn't get a job, and she could hardly sit around a house all day and do nothing. She was used to hard work.

The question was, if she wasn't going to pursue a career in entertainment anymore, what else could she do? She'd left high school with a diploma and no specific skills. She wasn't a secretary, or a teacher, or anything else useful, for that matter. All she knew how to do, other than act, was what she was doing now. Run a ranch household. And she couldn't imagine there was much of a market out there for that.

She rode out to where the ranch road met the highway. The big bull Day had warned her about was grazing in one of the front pastures again. Day had explained that they kept him pretty close to home, since he was too valuable a stud to risk on the range. The mail had been delivered, she noticed. Mindful of the bull's hulking presence, she stayed in the saddle as she collected the letters and magazines in the big metal box.

One was a sturdy brown envelope from her agent. She'd finally broken down and told Karl how to reach her, after he'd promised not to call unless she called him first. The envelope looked familiar. Fan mail. She received these collected letters once or twice a week in a mass. If she wasn't diligent about answering each letter, the stack could pile up to an impossibly daunting height. Rats. She'd planned on starting a new mystery novel this evening. Looked as if she would be answering fan mail instead. If these people took the time to write to her she felt obligated to write back.

Glancing at her watch, she realized she'd be answering a lot more than that if she didn't get back and get cracking on dinner.

She was turning into a pretty damned good cook, Day thought later that evening. The lasagna had really hit the spot, especially when it was paired with that homemade Italian bread Angel had baked. And the dessert hadn't hurt any, either. An unwilling smile tugged at his lips as he recalled the expression on the ranch hands' faces when Angel had uncovered the trays of cream puffs.

"What'n tarnation's that?" old Wes had grumbled. "Whatever happened to shoofly pie?"

"I haven't made shoofly pie in years," Angel had responded. "But I'll try one tomorrow just for you." Her smile had melted more than one man into a willing puddle on the floor, and when she urged them to "just try one bite" of the cream puffs, not a man had complained further. Their expressions, as the sweet confection had dissolved in their mouths, had been akin to discovering heaven on earth.

The cream puffs *had* been delicious. And the baking activity had been exactly what Beth Ann had needed to take her attention off the fact that her beloved Aunt Dulcie had departed for Albuquerque right before dinner. Angel had deflected that tantrum, too, he remembered as he idly picked up the mail that had been laid on his desk. Beth Ann had been so excited about drizzling chocolate sauce over the cream puffs that she'd completely forgotten to cry when Dulcie left.

A buff-colored envelope caught his eye and he slit it open, prepared to toss it immediately if it was, as he suspected, junk mail. His eyes narrowed as he read the letterhead of his ex-wife's lawyer. A moment later, he sat straight in his chair. *Assess his life-style, hell!*

Hardly knowing what he was doing, he rose and left the office. Beth Ann was in bed and he thought Angel had settled down in the living room for the evening.

"You're not going to believe this," he said, finding her seated cross-legged on the couch as he barged into the room.

She jumped visibly, and the envelope she was holding by one corner dropped to the floor. A sound of distress escaped her.

He took a step nearer, his own trouble forgotten. "Are you all right?" It was apparent that she wasn't. Her face was white and her dark eyes looked enormous... and scared. No, not scared, *terrified*. Terrified? What, he wondered, could put that look on the face of an immensely wealthy actress at the top of her profession? Belatedly he realized she hadn't answered him. He crossed the room and sat on the couch beside her. "Hey." He waved a hand before her eyes. "What's the matter?"

She still didn't answer. Slowly her gaze swung to his. Equally slowly she raised a hand and pointed to the envelope that had fluttered to the floor.

He reached down to pick it up and that seemed to break the spell.

"Be careful," she said. "You don't want to erase any fingerprints."

Startled, he glanced at her to see if she was teasing him. She wasn't smiling, wasn't kidding in the least. Digging into his pocket, he fished out the clean bandanna he'd put there after he'd showered and changed. Then he bent and gingerly snagged the envelope by the corner as he'd seen her holding it. He had a letter opener in his office and he swiftly retrieved it and slit the top, then carefully shook out the single sheet of paper onto the couch beside Angel.

She gave no indication of wanting to read it. Indeed, when he laid it near her, she recoiled visibly.

He eyed her, then the letter. He really shouldn't invade her privacy. But on the other hand, she looked like she needed some help dealing with whatever it was. He was her host. Wasn't it his obligation to take care of her?

Decision made, he caught an edge of the letter between his cloth-covered thumb and forefinger and held it up. As it fell open, he could see that it had been printed on a computer or typewriter. Angel made another small, involuntary sound of distress, which drew his gaze again. If she lost any more color, he thought, she'd match the sheet of paper in his hand.

Turning his attention back to it, he quickly skimmed the short message. As he read, he felt his stomach clench at the filthy phrases and the possessive tone.

Whoever had written this had a very, very sick mind.

Tossing the letter down on the coffee table with his bandanna, he took Angel's hands in his. They felt like two blocks of ice. "Do you get a lot of fan mail like that?" he asked incredulously.

She shook her head.

Then it struck him that she'd known what it was before he'd opened it. She'd known as soon as she'd seen it. "Have you gotten letters like this one before?" He realized he was rubbing his thumbs across her knuckles, unconsciously trying to warm her cold fingers, and he forced himself to relax.

Angel nodded. "I've been receiving them for nearly a year now."

A year! He was thunderstruck. "Have you told the police? They ought to be able to stop him."

Her mouth lifted in a sad parody of a smile. "Oh, the police know. In fact, they have a whole collection of these letters." Her voice quivered and she stopped for a moment. He could almost see her gathering her strength to prevent herself from breaking down altogether. "Do you have any idea of how strained the resources of the L.A. police are? This person hasn't harmed me...yet. I've never seem him, never had any contact other than these letters and some phone calls."

"But this is a form of stalking, isn't it?"

She nodded. "I suppose if he's ever caught, they could charge him with that. But who's going to catch him? The police have a lot more serious problems than this. They suggested I hire a bodyguard." She made a wry grimace. "Hardly inspired my confidence."

"What about a private investigator? Someone who is working solely for you?" He couldn't believe there wasn't a way to stop the creep who was sending her this stuff.

"They suggested that, too." Her tone was flat, dismissive, telling him what she'd thought of the idea.

Her attitude made no sense to him, and his impatience colored his tone. "I don't get it. You'll take a chance on having some nut hurt you just because you don't want to spend the money on a bodyguard or an investigator?"

"Money has nothing to do with it!" Color tinged her too-pale cheeks. "It's...privacy. I can't bear the thought of hiring someone to dig into my life under the guise of helping me. Or of hiring someone to follow me around. I told you I wanted to leave public life, but I didn't tell you *all* the reasons why. This is the big one." Her voice rose. "I can't bear the thought of living the rest of my life in a fishbowl, having the world know every move I make, and especially having to fear that I'll attract the attention of someone who's... unbalanced.''

"Okay, okay, calm down. I'm sorry I brought it up.'' Her voice had risen to such a pitch that he was afraid she might wake Beth Ann. He put an arm around her shoulders and patted awkwardly, not sure what kind of comfort she'd accept from him after the...misunderstandings they'd continually had. And, if it came down to it, not sure how big a dose of proximity to her his body could take. His mind might know that she was the wrong kind of woman for him, but that didn't stop the cut of his jeans from becoming almighty tight every time he spent more than a minute near her.

She heaved an enormous sigh and her tense body relaxed a little, conforming to his contours. His body reacted as he'd known it would, and he slipped his hand more firmly down her arm and pulled her closer. Might as well enjoy a few minutes of torture, even though he knew it could go no further. He turned his head and rested his chin against her temple, amazed at how such a simple action could stir up so many emotions. He missed this almost as much as he missed the steady sex that his marriage had ensured.

In the beginning, he and Jada had had moments like this, moments of sweet security when her mere presence had soothed something inside him. But it hadn't lasted long, he recalled. He could probably count on one hand the days his marriage had been either sweet or secure.

Deliberately he shoved away the distracting thoughts and concentrated on this moment, and on Angel. Her hair smelled of the sweet confections she'd whipped up for dessert. Good enough to eat ... *That* thought ushered in a host of disturbingly provocative mental images that quickened his pulse and made him shift uncomfortably.

Hell, he thought. *You need to get involved with her just about as bad as you need a hole right through your forehead. Forget it. She's trouble with a capital* T.

Trouble. The word brought to mind his reason for seeking her out in the first place, and he realized uncomfortably that it hadn't even occurred to him *not* to share the news of Jada's machinations with her.

The letter he'd brought into the room lay discarded on the coffee table. Withdrawing his arm from around her, he gave a mirthless grunt as he leaned forward to retrieve it. "Guess the mailman must have had it in for us today. Look what came for me."

She stirred and sat up straighter, creating space between them. Then she took the letter from him as if it might burn her fingers. "What's this?"

"Read it."

She did. Her finely drawn eyebrows knit together first in puzzlement, then in rising anger, and her expression mirrored his angry incredulity when she raised her gaze to him again. "She's hired a caseworker to assess your lifestyle? You don't have to submit to that, do you?"

Day shrugged. "If I don't, it sounds like they're prepared to get a court order."

"What exactly does this involve?"

He indicated the second sheet protruding from the envelope. "The first visit will be a formal, scheduled one that includes an interview. Then this ... caseworker is going to show up without giving any notice three more times for what they call 'informal' visits. Guess they'll be hoping to catch me doing something wrong."

"I would hope that this caseworker will be objective." Angel frowned thoughtfully. "Do you get any input on who it is?"

"Nope."

"Can you insist on getting a caseworker to report on Jada?"

His eyebrows rose in approval as he snapped his fingers. He hadn't thought of that. "I imagine I could. Good idea." He rose. "I'll go call my lawyer right now."

"Isn't it getting late?" Angel rose to her feet and gathered her papers.

"Not for something this important." He picked up his letter. Then he noticed the other one—hers—still lying on the table. He gestured toward it. "What should we do with this?"

"Oh." She looked as if she'd temporarily forgotten it, which pleased him immensely. "It should be sealed in a plastic bag and sent to the police...the L.A. police, I suppose, since it came with a batch of fan mail that I received today from my agent."

"I'll take care of it."

"Thank you. Good night."

Her eyes were shadowed, her classic cheekbones enhanced by the patterns of light and dark that played across her face in the lamplight. As she mounted the stairs, he couldn't restrain himself from hungrily assessing the way she filled out her jeans. She might be fashionably slender, but what little padding she had was certainly attached in the right places. And how.

Double hell. Another thought struck him and he scowled automatically. His chances of retaining custody of Beth Ann were dicey and he knew it. What would this damned social worker think when she visited his home and saw Angel, to whom he wasn't married or related, in residence? The woman was too damned gorgeous for him to pass off as a housekeeper. It was going to look improper no matter how he tried to explain.

If only Dulcie hadn't had to leave. Intuition told him his sister's marriage wasn't in the best of conditions. Begging her to stay wouldn't have accomplished anything except forcing her to choose between her family and that skirt-chasing husband of hers. Nothing would make him happier, Day thought, than to have the chance to explain to Lyle Meadows what fidelity meant.

Preferably with his fists.

But Dulce was a big girl now, and he had too many problems of his own to deliberately mess in her life. What the hell was he going to do about these so-called inspections that Jada had managed to subject him to? Without a wife, his life-style was going to look bad even to the most reasonable judge....

A wife. That was it. He needed a temporary wife.

The idea delighted him no end. He could practically envision a cardboard wife whom he moved into position for the visits.... His good mood faded. If only it could be that easy. Still, it *might* work. He'd have to give this notion some serious thought.

There was going to be a dance next Saturday night in Deming. He normally hated those things, but he'd make an appearance, scout out the available women. Stranger things had happened. Maybe one of them would agree to be a short-term wife.

A sound woke Angel in the middle of the night. At least, she thought it must be the middle of the night since her room was pitch-dark. She heard the noise again—a scuffling sound that instantly filled her with fear. She reached for the container of repellent spray she'd kept at her bedside for the past year.

But her groping hand encountered only the spare lines of the Southwestern-style bedside table and something that felt like a... Book. Her book. Memory returned. She wasn't in L.A. She was in New Mexico. On the Red Arrow Ranch to be exact.

The sound came again and she flipped back her covers and reached for her robe in the same motion. Was it Beth Ann? Hurrying into the hallway, she nearly rammed into Day coming out of his room.

"What's wrong?" she blurted, trying to get past him. "Is Beth Ann awake?"

He captured her elbows, preventing her from moving into the child's room. She realized he was fully dressed.

"Shh. She's sound asleep, far as I know. One of the men just paged me. There's a mare down in a bad labor and I've got to get out to the barn fast."

She shook her head, trying to assimilate the information. "Okay. What can I do?"

"Go back to bed." He released her and swung away.

She shook her head and hurried back to her room for something to wear, knowing he could be in for a long night. "I'll bring you some coffee."

Six

Angel had been right. It was a long night. While Day stomped into his boots on the back porch and went on out to the barn, she started a pot of coffee. Yawning, she leaned against the counter while she waited for the coffee to perk.

It was funny how easily she'd slipped back into the rhythms of ranch routine. She'd been away from New Mexico for nearly seven years, but already she felt as if she'd never been away.

Well, almost. If it wasn't for the palpable aura of danger that she could practically feel sometimes, she'd be content. Contentment was a strange word to apply to the backbreaking labor that went into keeping a house going on a working ranch, she thought with a wry smile, but it did indeed apply.

When Angel was a child, her mother had worked in the houses on several ranches where her father had taken work. Then after her mother had died, her father had drifted from ranch to ranch for a while. By the time they'd landed in Deming when she was a teenager, she'd been old enough to help with housework. The housekeeper at the Double Dos, where her father was a hand, had been a crusty soul with a marshmallow interior. She'd taken Angel under her wing and taught her everything she knew, from cooking to cleaning and everything in between. Angel's adolescence had been a painless affair—she'd been a late bloomer and boys had barely noticed her. She'd barely noticed them, either. Riding and roping when she wasn't in school and helping with housekeeping the rest of the time left little time for boy-craziness.

The coffee stopped dripping, and she brought a thermos out of the pantry and filled it with quick, deft motions. Then, shrugging into a sheepskin jacket that, judging from the way her wrists protruded from the sleeves, belonged to Dulcie, she pocketed the portable child monitor on the kitchen counter and headed for the barn. If Beth Ann woke, she could be back in the house within a minute.

She pulled open the heavy door and slipped quietly into the barn, blinking in the blackness. It was much darker in here than it had been outside, where a billion stars were visible in the sky. As her eyes adjusted, she could see a faint light coming from a box stall about halfway down.

Day was on the floor of the stall beside a sweating mare. The horse's eyes rolled occasionally but she was too weak to do more than that, even when another contraction hit. Angel perched on a high crossbar, out of the way of the men who were working with Day. She watched, tears slipping down her face as they brought a limp, lifeless foal into the world.

At the sound of an engine growling into the yard, Day glanced up at her. "That's the vet. Bring him in here." As she hurried to obey, she realized she hadn't even been sure he knew she was there until that moment.

She poured coffee for everyone while the vet examined the mare and administered medication. After a short while, the mare was back on her feet, pitifully nosing everything in sight looking for her stillborn baby. The sight was more than Angel could bear. Gathering up the coffee leftovers, she tossed everything into the basket she'd carried out to the barn earlier and prepared to return to the house. To her surprise, Day fell into step with her.

He was covered in gore from his futile efforts to save the foal and his face was grim with fatigue and frustration. Although he was silent, she thought she knew what he was thinking. As they entered the utility room, she said, "It wasn't your fault."

"It was." He shrugged out of the soiled shirt and hurled it into the sink with a fury born of helplessness. "I should have called the damned vet sooner. That foal might have survived."

"There was nothing wrong with your judgment. You heard what the vet said." She kept her voice steady and quiet, aware of the rage he was barely holding in check. "The foal was too early. It probably couldn't have lived anyway." As he started to unbuckle his belt, her eyes widened. She realized he was going to strip off all his filthy clothes right here. Funny, she'd done love scenes with actors wearing next to nothing that hadn't affected her half as much as the mere prospect of seeing Day nude. "I'll get you something to wear," she offered in a rush.

By the time she got back with a clean shirt and jeans, he'd tossed every stitch into the laundry and she could hear the shower running in the adjacent bathroom. She hung the clothing on the bathroom door, and as soon as the water stopped, she started the washer. Then she went out to the kitchen to refill the coffeepot. Dawn would be breaking in less than an hour and it would be time to start breakfast.

She sensed his presence in the kitchen before she turned from the sink. He was standing at the window looking out toward the barn, and she could see from the jumping muscle in his jaw that he was still flaying himself for not calling the vet sooner. Cradling a mug of coffee, she acted on instinct, moving to his side without giving herself time to think about why it wasn't wise.

Slipping an arm around his waist, she offered him the mug. He draped one arm over her shoulders without comment, accepting the mug and taking a deep swallow before looking down at her, his silver eyes piercing. Hastily she tore her gaze from his and lowered her face to rest against his shoulder. He canted his chin against her temple.

"Thanks," he said quietly.

The moment was so sweet it brought tears to her eyes. For just an instant, she allowed herself to wish for the impossible—to imagine that this feeling between them was real, that she could always be there for him when he needed her. She dared to stroke her palm up and down his back in a comforting gesture. "You're welcome."

The action pressed her against him by the smallest increment and suddenly the embrace changed. The air crackled with intense energy...sexual energy. Her body recognized it before her mind accepted it, softening against him in an invitation she hadn't planned but couldn't regret. Day drew back and scanned her face, tilting up her chin with a gentle, but inflexible hand. She stared back, too caught in her feelings to hide them from him.

His mouth was bracketed by harsh lines of fatigue and his damp hair quirked into short curls all over his head. Beneath her palm was hard, muscular flesh; along her side where she rested against him, spread a glowing heat.

Sexual attraction. She knew it for what it was. And if she was smart, she would go back to her work and forget him.

If only she could.

Slowly he moved to set the mug on the windowsill without ever breaking their eye contact. The arm around her shoulders tightened, the other settled at her hip, then slipped around her back to draw her against him. His eyes gave away his intent as slowly, surely, he lowered his head.

When his lips locked onto hers, her knees went weak. Perfect, was the last coherent thought her mind formulated. She hadn't permitted herself to think of kissing him after their last fevered encounter in her bedroom, but now every sensation came rushing back. Her arms slipped up around his neck as she willingly gave herself to the magic they made together.

She felt his hands fumbling with her ponytail, then her hair dropped loosely down her back. Immediately he spread the fingers of one hand and combed through the heavy mass, pulling it forward to anchor her against him.

Her breasts were crushed against his chest, her belly rubbed against his hard hips. She sucked in a gasp that was almost a moan.

And then he shoved her away.

She was so shocked she would have fallen if he hadn't held on to her forearms with an unbreakable grip. She couldn't speak, could barely think for all the messages that were crowding her brain.

Arousal, surrender, rejection, humiliation... It was that last that quickly grew to overshadow all else, sweeping over her in waves of mortification that sent deep, hot color to her face and brought tears to her eyes.

Oh, damn, she'd done it again. Hadn't he made it clear the last time that he didn't want her? His body might be willing, but his mind certainly didn't want any part of her. And she'd known it. But she wasn't like his ex-wife. Couldn't he see that?

Her knees were shaking and she wanted to cry. Badly. Instead, she bit her lip until she could taste blood, searching her mind for the right words, if there were any, that would end this unbearable moment.

His hands were still hard on her arms and she stepped away, shaking back her hair. She gestured helplessly. "Look, I—"

"Don't." He held up a hand. "It wasn't all your fault. But this...us...isn't what I want." He sounded desperate. "I've got enough problems right now—"

"And so do I." She seized on the word, though a part of her registered indignation that he should classify her as such. "Let's just forget this ever happened. In another week or two, you'll have a housekeeper and I'll be out of your hair for good."

Silence fell. She willed him to leave. Pride refused to allow her to be the one who broke and ran so she lifted her chin and stared him down.

Finally he shrugged and started for the door. Then, almost out, he halted and turned back to her. "Where will you go? What are you going to do?"

"That's not your problem," she said, throwing the words back in his face. "You've got enough to worry about."

At breakfast on Saturday, the ranch hands were a talkative bunch. Seemed there was going to be a dance in Deming in the evening and almost everyone on the ranch was going.

"Why don't you come along with us, Miss Angel?" Smokey proposed. "Them dances are a real good time. Lots of friendly folks around these parts."

"I don't think so—" she began, but when the others seconded the young hand's invitation, she gave in with a forced laugh. "If Day doesn't need me to help with Beth Ann, I guess I'll go." The last thing she was in the mood for was socializing, but surely there would be some folks there who would remember her father. Besides, it would certainly be better than the alternative, which was sitting in the living room alone while Day worked in his office and avoided her as carefully as she had sidestepped him all week.

And so at six o'clock that evening, she found herself jouncing into Deming in a pickup truck crammed with cowboys. "What time will we be coming home?" she asked. "And where shall I meet you?"

Wes grinned. "Ain't got no set schedule. Somebody'll hunt you up when we head home."

It wasn't the most satisfactory arrangement, but she guessed it would have to do.

Once inside the big hall where the dance was being held, she had no trouble locating several people whom she'd known during her youth in Luna County. She'd purposely worn her hair pulled back and omitted makeup again, and the small illusion worked its usual magic. She was able to divert the conversation from herself by simply saying she lived and worked in California now.

She chatted for an hour or so, then found herself besieged by the hands, every one of whom seemed to want to dance. The men were attentive, but when she declined, they respected her wishes and eventually their attentions wandered elsewhere. She found a perch on a hay bale in a quiet corner, where she simply sat, chin on knees, enjoying the colorful scene in the hall. Every so often, a cowboy caught her in his sights and came over to try to get her onto the dance floor, but she was firm though pleasant in refusing.

After one such episode, she glanced around the room suddenly feeling that she was being watched. When her gaze collided with Day's narrow-eyed appraisal, she felt the blood rush to her cheeks. She hadn't realized he was coming.

She didn't know what to expect, but when he turned his back and crossed the room to speak to a slender woman in a denim skirt, hurt creased her heart with an unexpected force. He hadn't asked her to come with him, hadn't even mentioned this dance to her. If there was any doubt in her mind about what kind of relationship was between them, it was now crystal clear. None.

He'd responded to the signals that she couldn't prevent herself from sending, though he'd drawn away of his own free will each time. He might be physically attracted to her, but that was it. He wasn't interested in anything more.

Her face burned. Any quiet pleasure she'd taken in the evening was gone. And it only went downhill from then on. She didn't stir from her corner again, not even to get a glass of punch. The ranch hands appeared to have forgotten her, which suited her in some ways, although she would have dearly loved to leave.

The room seemed to shrink in size after Day's arrival. Everywhere she looked, he seemed to appear. He danced with the woman in the denim skirt, and then several more. For a while, he lingered near the punch bowl, talking to several other men she thought were also ranchers. Wherever he was, she observed that the feminine activity around him practically doubled. Some of those women had to be married! And the rest... Why, that girl in the pink top couldn't be out of high school yet. She'd sashayed by Day at least four times, and once Angel had seen Day speak to the girl, tugging a lock of her auburn hair in a teasing manner.

Finally, just past eleven o'clock, she decided enough was enough. He couldn't have made it clearer that she was not his kind of woman. Slipping off the hay bale, she began to make her way around the fringe of the crowd. She deliberately kept her gaze aimed at the floor until she got to the far door. Most of the ranch hands had disappeared some time back. Maybe one of them was outside and would take her home if she asked.

She reached for the door, but as she threw her weight into pulling it open, a large hand slapped against the door, easily preventing her from opening it. "Where are you running off to? The night is young."

Angel gritted her teeth. She'd recognized Day's scent the moment he'd approached, even before he'd spoken. Slowly she turned around. Determined not to let him see that he'd ruined her evening, she looked at the floor as she said, "I'm going to hunt up one of the boys. I'm ready to go home now."

He didn't remove his hand from the door. In fact, he laughed. Laughed! She wanted to hit him.

"I suspect most of the boys are, uh, occupied for a few more hours. I don't really think you want to try hunting for any of them right now."

That startled her into lifting her head. "A few more hours? But I don't want to stay here that long." Belatedly she realized that he was implying that most of his men were involved in some hot and heavy romancing. "Oh. I see."

He laughed again, and even though she was furious with him, she couldn't help noticing how handsome he was, with his white teeth flashing against sun-darkened skin and— *Stop it, you stupid girl. How much more rejection do you need?* "Well," she said, "in that case, I guess I'll sit for another spell."

But as she ducked under his arm and turned away, he said, "I'll take you home if you're ready. Beth Ann has a baby-sitter and I wasn't going to stay much longer anyway."

"That's not necessary—"

"No, it's not, but I offered and I meant it."

"All right." Then, realizing she'd been less than gracious, she added, "Thank you."

Day smiled down at her. "Don't thank me yet. There's a price."

She dropped her efforts at courtesy and scowled. "What is it? I'm not in the mood for any more of your...games."

One of his eyebrows arched in response. "No games, Angel. Just a dance. All I'm asking is one single dance, and then I'll take you home."

Oh, she despised herself. She was so weak. She knew better, knew that tomorrow she'd be hurting and be sorry, but when he stood before her with that hopeful expression on his face, her common sense flew right off and left her with nothing but longing. "I guess so," she said. "Just one dance."

As luck would have it, it was a waltz. He pulled her firmly against him and swept her around the room to the slow, sweet rhythms of the dance, giving her no chance to argue or protest.

Did she ever feel good! Her soft body brushed against his in all the right places and he had to admit he was partial to spinning in tight circles because of the way it pressed her up against his all-too-eager hips. Had he been waiting for this all evening?

He'd known she was coming into town with the hands, and that he'd probably have to take her home. But what he hadn't realized was that she would ruin his concentration.

He'd come to this damned shindig with a purpose. Nearly every available woman in Deming came to these things. Now that he'd settled on this idea of a temporary marriage, all he needed to do was find a wife. Of course, he was going to have to be very careful about how he finessed this. It was imperative that whoever agreed to his proposal understand that the marriage would be annulled after he got custody of Beth Ann.

But now that he was here, with Angel in his arms, he realized two things. The first was that marriage to a local woman was out of the question. They'd expect a normal, till-death-do-us-part kind of marriage. And besides, he wasn't prepared to let the whole community be privy to his problems. If he asked a local woman to marry him temporarily, it would be all over Luna County in hours.

The second thing he realized was a whole lot less palatable. He was going to have to have Angel. Not necessarily in marriage, but writhing underneath him in bed for a very long time. Days, weeks even. He just couldn't fight it any longer.

No other woman had looked suitable to him tonight and he knew it wasn't simply because they were all from around Deming. No, it was because they weren't Angel. With her in his head he couldn't even focus on anyone else's face, much less consider inviting one of them to live in his house.

For the first time, he allowed himself to consider asking her to marry him. Only temporarily, of course. Of course. Anything else would be sheer insanity. As it was, he was begging for trouble, involving himself with another actress. But try as he might, he simply couldn't believe Angel had been tarred with the same brush as Jada. She'd pitched in at the ranch even before Dulcie had left, and since then she'd been as solid as a rock. He literally couldn't have gotten along without her. That was one plus—she was already becoming familiar with his routine.

Another was his daughter. Beth Ann knew Angel. She was already well on her way to being attached, and keeping Angel right where she was could only be good for his daughter. He purposely refused to think about how he'd deal with Bethie when Angel eventually left. By then, she should be secure enough that it wouldn't be such a wrench.

"I didn't see you on the dance floor tonight," he said against her ear. He felt a shiver run through her and he was gratified to realize that she was feeling it, too, these quivers of sexual excitement that had his insides all ajiggle.

"I didn't feel like dancing," she said. "I just wanted to watch all the people."

"I'm glad," he said, turning his head to nuzzle against her ear again. "I would have been jealous." He'd hoped for a reaction, but when she reared back and stopped dead in the middle of the dance floor, he hastily grabbed her and forced her into the dance pattern again. "What's the matter with you?" he growled.

"What's the matter with *me?*" Her voice shook and he didn't think it was with passion. "You kiss me senseless and then walk away—*twice*. You didn't invite me to this dance, remember? Not to mention the fact that you ignored me all evening while you were dancing with your little—little conquests, and now you're here seducing me with words. I don't get it. Am I a handy backup because nothing better came along?"

"Hell, no!" His voice came out louder and more impatient than he'd intended, and several other couples cast openly curious glances at them. He swore. "Let's get out of here. We need to talk."

Gripping her hand without giving her a choice, he towed her toward the door.

As he plowed through the crowd, an imperious voice caught his attention. "David Kincaid! You come over here and pay your respects, young man."

Reluctantly he swerved and slowed to pause beside one of the tables lining the room. "Good evening, Miss Ivy. It sure is nice to see you out and about."

"It's nice to see you, too, David. You're the spittin' image of your daddy, rest his soul." The old woman eyeballed Angel with blatant curiosity. "And who's this pretty little thing?"

Day suppressed a sigh. Ivy McClintock was the grand dame of Luna County ranching. She was also one of the biggest gossips he knew. Though he guessed it could be worse. At least she was generally kind with her gossiping.

"Mrs. McClintock, this is Angel...Vandervere. She used to live around here and she's been staying at the Red Arrow visiting Dulcie. Angel, Mrs. Ivy McClintock."

"Pleased to meet you, ma'am," Angel said.

"Vandervere? You Emmet's daughter?" Ivy might be pushing eighty, but her mind was as sharp as the day she'd celebrated her twenty-first.

"Yes, ma'am."

"Shame about that, him dyin' so young," Ivy pronounced. Then she peered at Angel. "You sure prettied up. Best I remember, you were a skinny little filly with eyes too big for the rest of your face."

"Thank you." Angel smiled at the old lady. "I think."

"Always wondered what happened to you. Just up and left one day. Heard you married some boy up Albuquerque way, and then nothing."

Angel's smile had dimmed to a carefully blank expression. He wondered what she was thinking, if Ivy's prying had dredged up some sadness—and then Ivy turned her gimlet-eyed speculation on him. "You say she's visiting Dulcie? Didn't see her here."

"No, ma'am. Dulcie had to go back upstate." As soon as the words were out of his mouth, he wanted to grab them back. Now why had he told her that? Soon all of Deming would know that he had a woman living at his ranch. He supposed that kind of thing shouldn't really blow anybody's skirt in this day and age, but he knew how small communities could turn a molehill into a mountain. Especially this small community.

Before Ivy could take her interrogation any further, he tipped his hat, snagging Angel's hand at the same instant. "It surely was nice to see you, Miss Ivy," he said. "If you'll excuse me, I have to get Angel home now. Good evening."

They made it to his truck without any more interruptions, but when he offered her his hand to help her in, she

ignored him and hoisted herself up, treating him to a view
of rounded bottom snugly encased in crisp new jeans. That
alone was enough to addle a man's brain, he decided,
walking around to the driver's side.

He drove the truck out of town and onto the highway
before he tried to talk to her. She huddled in the far corner with her arms crossed, studiously looking out the side
window at mile after mile of dark, flat land.

How to begin? From the way she'd jumped down his
throat in the dance hall, he wasn't sure trying to start a
conversation while he was driving was such a good idea.
But inside, a deep satisfaction began to expand. She'd been
furious with him on the dance floor, no question about it.
And it had sounded as if the reason she'd been so mad was
because she'd wanted more of his attention than she'd
gotten.

He liked the idea. He liked it a lot. He recalled his initial plans for a quiet, passionless marriage and an equally
quiet annulment. Now that he'd considered marrying Angel, he knew the other would never do. Oh, well. Divorce
was as easy as annulment, easier in some places. And
marriage to Angel, having her warm body available to him
every night, was a lure he could no longer resist.

The thought froze him in his mental tracks. He hadn't
been able to resist Jada, either. But that had been a whole
different story, he told himself firmly. Jada had been useless on the ranch. Angel had already proven she could
work. And she didn't want to deprive him of his daughter, either. In fact, marrying her would ensure that didn't
happen.

He let her sulk the whole rest of the way home. When he
pulled up in front of the ranch house, he started to shut off
the engine, then realized that she had opened her door and
was already climbing out.

"Hey, wait a minute." He grabbed at her and got his
fingers through the belt loops of her jeans, then unfas-

tened his seat belt and slid across toward her. "I want to talk to you."

"Too bad," she snapped over her shoulder, straining against his grip. "I don't have anything else to say to you. *Let me go!*"

"Not a chance." He dragged her back into the truck and her frantic clutch for the door handle neatly slammed the door shut again. The dome light went off at the exact instant he realized that he had a lapful of woman and he chuckled beneath his breath.

The sound must have infuriated her because she twisted and wriggled twice as frantically. "Damn you, Day Kincaid. I'm not one of your heifers to be wrestled into submission. I don't want to talk to you."

He felt his temper beginning to fray at the edges. This combative female wasn't the tranquil, soothing woman who quietly accomplished a lion's share of work in a day's time. As she continued to struggle, one hand came up and smacked him solidly in the chest.

That did it. Capturing that hand and her other one, which was about to make contact with his jaw, he gritted, "Okay, you don't want to talk, we won't talk." And he slammed his mouth down on hers.

Seven

She was like a twisty little mustang in his arms, writhing and heaving, trying to throw him off. The challenge fired his blood, and as he pinned her against him, he increased the intensity of the kiss, teasing her with his tongue until she quit bucking. Then, in a capitulation as unexpected as it was total, her body softened and she allowed him to pull her closer.

Immediately he took advantage of the concession, slanting his mouth more fully over hers and slipping his tongue deep inside. She squirmed against him and he released her hands, sliding his palm down her back to curve under her buttock and drape one leg over his thigh in a blatant intimacy that his body recognized and swelled to meet.

He kept one arm beneath her neck and slid backward, taking her with him across the seat, then slowly he eased her down until she lay almost full-length on the rough fabric bench. Her breasts were an enticement he'd resisted since the night in her room, and he knew he had to touch her. The blouse she wore was a pretty, ruffled thing with full sleeves and a wide, low collar; the promise of warm flesh beneath it made his fingers shake as he fumbled with the slippery buttons. The pace was fast and furious. She began to work open the buttons from the bottom up, baring creamy skin and a wisp of lacy brassiere so skimpy and transparent that he couldn't believe it had any useful purpose.

He wanted to comment on it, to tease her about her choice of lingerie, but his body was pulsing, pounding, the blood rushing through his temples, and no words would come. With a low groan, he inserted a finger in the shadowed valley between her breasts and tugged the bra down, trapping her arms in layers of strap and sleeve, baring her torso for his plunder.

She froze. So did he. In the moonlight that poured through the windshield, he could see that she was perfectly shaped, with high round breasts from which tiny nipples thrust forward in invitation. He held up his hand, palm out, and brushed it lightly back and forth, from one crest to the other.

She sucked in a sharp gasp, and the slender leg he'd drawn up over his thigh tightened around him. Anticipation twisted a knot tighter and he shifted, trying to relieve the discomfort in his jeans.

It didn't help.

His body knew what it wanted, and he eased his weight against her until his erection was pressed flush against her spread thighs. She whimpered. He groaned, thrusting forward rhythmically. Through the fabric of their clothing, the sensation was a sweet torment. His attention was claimed again by her exposed breasts, her pale flesh gleaming in the dim light. He lowered his head and took one nipple in a strong suckle.

She reacted as if he'd applied an electric shock. Her body jerked and she screamed. Her hands speared into his hair and forced him even closer. Aware that his own control was nearly gone, he shifted to one side, grappling with the snap of her jeans, oblivious to all but the need that drove him to uncover her deepest secrets and bury himself within her.

Then a bright light blinded him. It swept past in an instant, leaving him stunned and uncomprehending until the crunch of tires on stone pierced his state of shock. He knew what it was without looking to confirm the fact. The men were returning.

Damn! Hastily he sat up, dragging the edges of her blouse together and clutching them in one big first. He was too aroused to sit up completely, confined as he was by his damned jeans, and he had to sprawl along the seat. Angel squirmed her way from beneath him, which didn't do a thing to help him settle down. Shoving his hand away, she quickly buttoned her blouse again while he peered out the window at the approaching truck.

"Hey, Boss! Ever'thing all right in there?" The voice belonged to Wes.

"Just fine." His voice was a warning growl, but apparently it was lost on the hands.

A chorus of distinctly tipsy laughter floated across on the night air. "If it ain't," Joe-Bob called, chortling, "you just holler. We'd be 'bliged to help out."

Day's temper snapped and he reached for the door handle. "You're all gonna need help walking tomorrow if you don't get out of here pronto!"

They must have heard the grim note of truth ringing in his voice. Before he could make good on his threat, the other truck growled into gear, bouncing on down the driveway toward the bunkhouse.

At the same moment, he heard Angel's door open and slam again. He turned, but she was already out of the truck, running for the house. "Wait! I still want to talk to you," he hollered at her back. But he might as well not have bothered for all the notice she gave him. By the time he'd taken the keys out of the ignition, she was through the front door.

And unless he wanted to beat down her bedroom door and haul her out, he doubted he'd see her again tonight. For a minute, he almost considered dragging her into his room and into his bed and kissing every inch of that pale, silky body until she begged him for more.

His still-rigid flesh reacted to the thought and he groaned. It was going to be a hell of a long night.

Angel couldn't look him in the eye when he came into the kitchen the next morning. Instead, she busied herself preparing breakfast. She wanted to have it on the table before the men came in so she wouldn't have to see any of them. She still felt embarrassed.

And ashamed. It seemed Day Kincaid had to do nothing more than throw a few crumbs of his considerable charm her way before, bingo, she fell into his arms like a flower dropping petals. The worst part was that she couldn't even blame Day. She'd been a more-than-willing participant during the heated moments in the truck last night. Any opposition she'd thrown in his face had disappeared the minute he'd kissed her.

"Angel?" Day's voice was slightly impatient, as if he'd spoken her name more than once.

"Yes?" She concentrated on counting out flatware. Forget that kiss!

"We never talked last night."

She felt her face flame and she didn't dare look up. "There's nothing to talk about."

His boots were loud on the kitchen floor as he stepped to her side. She felt his hand slip beneath her chin, then he lifted her face for his inspection. "Yes," he said, "there is." At the sound of the door slamming and boots scuffling on the porch, a grimace crossed his face. "But we can't talk now. Tonight. In my office. As soon as Beth Ann is asleep."

She couldn't read anything in the gaze he leveled at her. But she knew what he was going to say as she watched him leave the room. And she agreed.

She couldn't stay here anymore.

A thrill of icy fear trickled down her spine to mingle with the misery that the thought of leaving had produced. She'd felt so safe ... so anonymous here. With her fair coloring unadorned by stage makeup, she'd faded into the background enough so that no one other than Day had made the connection to Angelique Sumner. She'd felt incredibly free for the past week. So free that for hours at a time she'd nearly forgotten her life could be at risk from a madman.

Now all those fears came rushing back.

Surely she could disappear. She had enough money to last her several lifetimes if she invested it and wasn't frivolous. She could even leave the country, start somewhere else with a new name. Leave all her troubles behind.

Leave Day Kincaid, and his darling daughter, and Dulcie and everyone else who had become such an important part of her life.

No. She couldn't do it. But she could, and should leave the Red Arrow while she still had the chance to do so without anyone being the wiser. She'd just go to Albuquerque and take the first plane out. What did it matter where she landed?

It didn't, if Day wasn't there.

The realization slipped into her conscious mind without fanfare. She'd been attracted to Day since she'd arrived at the ranch. She'd seen him working right along with his men, juggling finances and accounts, helping with housework. She'd seen him competently parenting his daughter and hurting at the thought that he might lose her.

He was rough and rugged, tender and gentle, principled and honest to a fault.

And she loved him. The flatware slipped from her fingers and she braced her palms on the counter. She loved him.

She was in the office waiting when he came down from putting Beth Ann to bed that night. Her stomach was in knots. She hadn't felt this sick at heart since the day she'd walked away from the adoption office and left her child to be comforted by strangers. Dully, she wondered how much more she would be expected to give up in this lifetime.

Day cleared his throat and she looked up to see him standing in the doorway. "Thank you for coming," he said formally.

He looked handsome with his dark hair freshly washed and a leather vest worn over his dark shirt, but his eyes kept darting around the room every time she looked his way.

She knew just how he felt. Having a civilized conversation was difficult enough without recalling the way they'd been rolling around in the truck last night, the way she'd let him do anything he pleased without even a token protest. He was probably worried that she had read too much into it, that she was going to start making demands and claims that he'd have to fend off. She felt the sting of mortification flushing her cheeks and she rushed into speech to cover it. "I have something I want to tell you, too," she said.

If he'd heard her, he gave no indication. "You know about the threat my ex-wife made, and this social worker she's sicced on me, right?"

"Yes, but—"

"Well, my lawyer has figured out a way to outfox her."

That caught her attention. "How?"

He grinned at her, a slow, easy shift of facial muscles that shouldn't make her knees weak or her heart beat faster. It shouldn't, but it did. "I'm going to get married."

Married. She felt as if someone had punched a fist right into her stomach. Though a giant hand was squeezing her rib cage and she couldn't get enough air, she murmured, "Congratulations."

As he was about to speak again she held up a hand before the tears could fall. "I know what you're trying to find a way to tell me and you're right. My presence would be incredibly awkward to explain to your...your fiancée. If you can give me a day or two to pack and make travel arrangements, I'll be gone as soon as I can."

"Can I finish?" He was still grinning, though his eyes were searching, looking for something...what?

It hurt her to look at him, knowing she was leaving and she wondered why he was so insistent. "I don't think we need to dissect last night," she whispered, looking away so he wouldn't see her falling apart. "It happened, it's over—"

"Dammit, woman! Will you quit yammering for two minutes?" Day put his hands on his hips and glared at her. "I'm trying to ask you to be my wife."

"Ask me...?" She was so shocked she couldn't finish the sentence.

He smiled grimly. "Yeah. You. Who else in this neck of the country would agree to marry me for a few months? The local women would expect it to be permanent and I don't want to be saddled with a wife for the rest of my life."

The words stung, even as she glimpsed heaven waiting. He wanted her—but only for a limited time. Could she live with that? Then another thought struck her. "But you read the tabloids. You even believed them. What if my supposed reputation causes trouble with your bid for custody?''

He snorted. "Compared to Jada Barrington's exploits, which I can prove are true, you're lily-white. Besides—" He shrugged. "How's she going to know my Angel is Angelique Sumner?''

She hesitated. He made it sound so easy. And she desperately wanted to leap up and shout yes. But logic held her back. This would never work.

"You're an actress," he said, apparently reading her hesitation as refusal. "Just consider it another role. Wife and mother.''

Slowly, she said, "I suppose it would give me more time..." *Time with you. Time for my heart to well and truly break.*

"You'd have plenty of time to think about where you want to go from here." He was beginning to sound desperate, and she found she liked it. "Please think about it, Angel. I need you. And you need me. You've been safe here. I've seen you relax a little more each day. No one can find you. If you become Mrs. David Kincaid, it will be that much easier to stay out of sight. And when the marriage ends, you'll have a new name—my name. You can start over anywhere you like without being tracked down.''

Everything he'd said was true. But still she hesitated. Only moments ago she'd been prepared to make a clean break. Wouldn't it be better for her to get the break over and done with so she could begin learning to live without him?

Suddenly, she became aware that he was standing right in front of her. He placed his hands on her shoulders and the sweet shock of his touch seared her through her clothing. "If we marry," he said, looking at her mouth, "it will be a real marriage in every way there is.''

She shuddered, trying not to let his touch eradicate her common sense. "But you don't trust me. You don't even particularly like me."

He moved his hands down to her hips and pulled her purposefully against him. "Does this feel like I don't like you?" The action made no secret of his arousal thrusting against her soft stomach. As always, she found it impossible to think when he was touching her. She dropped her forehead against his chest. He bent his head, pressing his mouth to the side of her neck. His lips were warm and wet as if he'd just licked them. "I trust you to be a good mother to Beth Ann," he whispered.

Well, that was something. *I need you,* he'd said. But he hadn't meant that he needed her in any deep personal sense. He needed her to help him save his daughter.

Then he touched his lips to hers and it ceased to matter. If she could be here with him—for him—she was going to stay.

The kiss had begun gently, but when she sighed and pressed herself against him, it was as if he threw off the restraints he'd imposed on himself. His mouth hardened, parting her lips. She raised her arms to circle his neck, spreading her fingers and combing through his damp curls with urgent pleasure. She was shameless, arching her body against his, thrilling to the feel of his hard loins. He made a low, rough noise deep in his throat as he slid his arms around her and held her fast to him, smoothing one big hand down her back and over the swell of her bottom to cup and mold the soft flesh there.

Then, holding her tight against him like that, as if he wanted to absorb her right into himself, he said, "This is what our marriage will be. It won't be platonic, and it can't be permanent, but it sure as hell can be great while it lasts." He leaned his forehead against hers, and she had to close her eyes at the intense communication he demanded. "Say yes."

"Yes." She breathed the word against his lips.

"I'll give you twenty-four hours to decide."

"Yes."

"We can put a time limit on it if that would make you feel—"

She kissed him, hard. "Yes."

Silence. Then, "You'll marry me?"

"Yes!" She blushed at how easy a mark she'd been, but he finally reacted.

"Well, hot damn!" His mouth rocked onto hers with all the finesse of a rutting bull for one glorious, grinding kiss, then he drew away again. "You won't be sorry." Keeping one arm around her, he urged her over to the calendar on the desk. "If I can get it all organized, we can get married on Friday," he said, tapping a finger on the day in question.

"Friday? That's too soon." Nerves tightened her throat and she swallowed. She'd expected to have plenty of time to reconcile herself to this decision.

"Considering the show we put on for the hands last night, I think we should marry as soon as possible. I don't want anybody snickering behind your back." His tone was sober, but he was smirking.

"It wasn't funny," she said. "Another few minutes and we'd have been...they'd have caught us..." There was no polite way to say it.

"Yeah." His drawn-out agreement barely suppressed his amusement. "Bare naked in the moonlight."

Her mouth twitched as he settled himself on the edge of the desk and drew her around to stand between his spread thighs. How could she be so embarrassed and still want to laugh? "I'll never be able to look those guys in the eye again," she said mournfully.

"Who cares?" He ran his hands up her back in a smooth caress. A second later, she felt a slight tug, and she realized that somehow he'd managed to open the clasp on

her bra! Did he know it? A swift glance up through her
lashes told her immediately that he did indeed know it.

She reached her arms behind her, fumbling to reclasp it
through the material of her shirt. "Great party trick," she
said dryly. "How many girls did you go through perfect-
ing that?"

He grinned. "Dozens. Only trouble is, it always breaks
the mood, just like this. Then again—" He surveyed her
as she stood with her arms back, breasts thrust against the
thin fabric as she arched her back, "—maybe it's worth
it."

Her cheeks felt like they were on fire. She made a face
at him before she turned her back, but he stepped up behind her.

"Don't be shy," he said, linking his arms around her
waist and pulling her back against him. "You have a
beautiful body." His mouth sought the sensitive flesh beneath her ear and she automatically tilted her head to give
him better access, leaning back against him.

He'd asked her to marry him—for a few months. If that
was all she was going to have, she was going to grab every
moment.

He slipped his hands up to cup her breasts through her
clothing, brushing his thumbs back and forth over her
nipples in a steady rhythm, sending shock waves of need
washing through her. In her abdomen, muscles began to
contract in an ever-tightening knot that urged her to shift
back and forth seeking relief. When he nipped at her neck,
the sharp sting of his teeth sent a jagged arrow of desire
straight to the quivering center of her.

Gasping, she put her hands behind her to grasp his but-
tocks and pull him close against her body. He lifted his
head, a deep groan escaping from down in his chest. "Let's
go upstairs," he breathed against her neck.

"All right." She laid her hands over his as he kneaded
her breasts. Under her palms, his hands stilled. Then he

turned her to him, catching her beneath the knees and sweeping her into his arms so quickly that she gave a startled squeak. Before she could protest, he strode out of the office toward the stairs. She remembered her resolve: *Enjoy it while it lasts.*

Relaxing, she laid her head against his shoulder, inhaling deeply. He'd showered just before supper as usual, and his skin exuded the clean, slightly soapy smell of healthy man. Pressing an experimental kiss against the side of the tanned column of flesh, she lingered, enjoying the firm, resilient give of his skin and the slight roughness of newly shaved beard.

Beneath her lips, his Adam's apple bobbed as he swallowed. "You little tease."

Immediately her confidence vanished. Was he pleased or annoyed with her? As he surged up the steps and elbowed open the door of her room, she rested her head passively against him. She'd had so little practice at this—either during or since her brief marriage—that she was too unsure of herself to make another overture.

Moving directly to her bed without bothering to turn on a light, he laid her on the quilt, coming down beside her before she had time to worry about what to do next. His fingers made short work of the buttons on her shirt, then he was pulling handfuls of it free of her jeans. Smoothing the fabric away from her body, he pushed her still-unfastened bra out of the way and deliberately lowered his lips to one taut tip.

"Oh!" Her body tightened in automatic response. Without thinking, she put her hands up to cradle his head and draw him closer. He eased his weight over her; she arched upward in response to his urgent domination.

Dark shadows filled the room. Only the scant moonlight filtering through the two windows relieved the total blackness. It wrapped them in a hushed dance of passion that heightened every brush of sensation, every glide of

skin over skin, every whisper of silky fabric falling away
from flesh.

She floated in a world where only his touch mattered,
her body tensing, twisting, driven onward to an inescapable conclusion. His hand slipped over the soft flesh of her
bared belly, rubbing smooth, rhythmic circles that gradually inched lower and lower, combing through the crisp
curls that protected vulnerable treasures....

"Wait." She grabbed his wrist, holding his hand from
its goal only because he allowed her to stop him. Reason
rushed back in a cold deluge that left her gasping. How
could she have forgotten? "We need...I'm not...
protected."

"Oh. I figured you were on the Pill." He stared blankly
at her for a moment, then dipped his head and pressed a
brief kiss against her lips. Rolling aside, he lay back and
crossed his hands behind his head. "Go ahead, honey. I'll
wait. But hurry back."

She sat up, bewildered, staring at him stretched out on
the bed. Then it began to dawn on her that he was expecting her to go and...and *prepare* herself. "But I don't
have—"

"Oh, hell." He sat up, too. "You mean you don't have
any protection?"

He sounded shocked, and she suddenly realized that
what she'd told him about her life-style hadn't registered
completely. Or maybe he just plain didn't believe her. He
clearly thought she would carry birth-control measures as
a matter of course, because she needed them often enough
to make it a given that she would protect herself. Anger
began to rise as she said, "I *told* you those tabloid articles
were out-and-out lies."

Wariness sprang into his eyes as he read the irritation in
her tone. "Now relax. I wasn't insinuating—"

"Hah!" She sprang off the bed, twisting the tails of her
shirt into a knot between her breasts that effectively cov-

ered everything vital. His Southwestern accent had thickened, as it always did in times of stress, slurring his words into lazy syllables, but this time she refused to be charmed. "You think I do this so much that I automatically take care of—"

"The problem is, I don't have anything, either."

Her eyebrows rose. She couldn't resist the chance to pay him back in kind. "Now that *is* amazing."

Reading her skepticism correctly, he said, "Not that amazing. I don't have time for much fooling around."

"Fooling around! Is that what you consider this?" Hurt provoked her into blurting out the question before she could stop it.

The tension in the room was heavy enough to smother them. A sob rose in her throat and she whirled away from the bed to stare out the window, choking back the sound.

He'd been sitting on the edge of the bed with one long leg dangling down, his shirt hanging open. Now she heard him get to his feet and come to stand behind her. When his hands cupped her shoulders, she reluctantly allowed him to turn her to face him.

He simply stared at her for a long moment, silver eyes probing her face in the dim light. Finally he said, "I'm not sure what I consider this. But you're right. It isn't just fooling around."

"Day, I—"

"Shh." He smiled a little, placing a finger across her lips. The contact stilled her instantly and he continued. "I wasn't entirely truthful with you or myself when I decided no local woman would do for a wife. The real truth is that when I looked around at that dance, I couldn't even see anybody else. Everywhere I looked, you got in the way." His face hardened a little. "I want you. For a good long time. Nobody else will do. I don't know exactly what's happening here, but I'm willing to take a chance on finding out." His hands slipped down her arms to enfold her fingers within his and his gaze was so piercing she could barely sustain the contact. "Are you willing to find out with me?"

Her heart beat a rapid tattoo of hope within her breast. He'd just offered her more than she'd allowed herself to believe in. With his admission came a springing joy, a prayer that desire could turn to love. She nodded.

He heaved a sigh and drew her into his arms, kissing her temple. She felt his heavy arousal still full against her, and without thinking she lightly brushed her hips against him.

His loud groan startled her. "Woman, you're going to kill me," he said ruefully. A wry grin tilted up the corners of his strong mouth. "This is the first time I can't do what I want because neither of us has any protection." He sobered and eyed her consideringly. "You suppose any of the hands would let me have a few condoms?"

Her eyes flew wide. "You wouldn't dare! Would you?"

He laughed at the sudden doubt in her tone. "No, I guess not. Friday is only two days away. I can wait until we get to town and we can buy what we want. Then we'll have us a real wedding night."

She blushed in the dark, glad he couldn't see her face as he kissed her quick and hard, then set her away from him.

"I'm getting out of here while I can still let you go," he said, and his voice went husky and low. "Friday can't come fast enough for me."

On Friday morning Angel donned a slim aqua suit, one of the few dressy items she'd brought to the ranch. Beth Ann was freshly bathed and dressed in a white eyelet float with tiny crinolines beneath it, and she fidgeted impatiently as Angel came into her bedroom and brushed her shining ebony curls.

"I'm glad you're going to be my mommy," she announced.

Angel smiled and knelt to hug the little girl. "I'm glad, too."

"I bet nobody else has an angel for a mommy. That makes me lucky!" She frowned thoughtfully, then her brow cleared and she smiled back at Angel. "Now you can fix it so that I can always stay with Daddy."

Angel's hands froze in the middle of buckling tiny black patent leather Mary Jane shoes. She forced herself to react casually. "Honey, I'm not a real angel. It's just my name."

Beth Ann was silent for a moment. Then she curled her hand trustingly into Angel's. "But if Daddy and me have you now, I don't need any other mommy, do I?"

Angel felt her heart shrink into a small, hard ball. What kinds of things could a woman do to make her child wish she didn't exist? Carefully she said, "Honey, you know you have another mommy. I'm sure she loves you very much."

"But I don't want to live with her!" There was a note of cornered desperation in the child's voice that brought tears to Angel's eyes.

"You live *here*," was all she could say as she picked up the child and rocked her. Beth Ann threw small arms around Angel's neck and squeezed with all her strength. Over the little girl's head, she saw Day standing in the doorway, his mouth set in a grim line.

"Forever?" Beth Ann demanded.

He stepped forward, laying one big hand soothingly on his daughter's back. "Forever," he confirmed.

"Daddy!" Beth Ann reached for him, her fears apparently allayed. "Angel and me are ready to get married now."

He took her from Angel's arms and settled her comfortably in one arm before extending his other to Angel. "Then let's go make it official."

Eight

They drove into Deming. On the way to the courthouse, Day pulled into the parking lot of a florist's shop. "Be back in a minute," he promised. And he was. As he climbed back into the sedan that he'd taken out of the garage that morning, he tossed several items into her lap. "Here. There's something for everybody."

"What's this?" She stared in surprise at the blossoms filling her lap as pleasure bloomed in her chest. There were two bouquets of fragrant white roses and lilies of the valley accented by dark, waxy leaves and cascading ferns. One was done in miniature and she handed it back over the seat to Beth Ann. "Look, honey. Daddy brought us flowers."

"Pretty, Daddy. Thank you," the little girl added when Angel slanted her a meaningful glance over her shoulder.

Day looked amused when she turned back to him. "These are beautiful," she said softly, so touched that she could barely speak. "Thank you."

If she didn't know better, she'd think the dull red crawling up his neck was embarrassment. "You're welcome," he said without turning his head toward her again. "There's a flower in a little bag there for my lapel, too."

When they arrived at the courthouse, she found that he wasn't finished with surprises. Waiting to greet them in the hallway was a familiar figure.

"Aunt Dulcie!" squealed Beth Ann, running ahead of them to be scooped up. "We didn't knowed you were here."

"It was a last-minute decision," Dulcie said, smiling at Angel over Beth Ann's head.

"I'm so glad you came." Angel felt tears pricking at the backs of her eyes and she smiled tremulously as she hugged her friend. "It means a lot to have you with us today." She didn't like the way Dulcie looked, even more thin and pale than she'd been at the ranch, but she sensed from the brittle, determined smile that Dulcie gave her that there would be no explanations today.

"It's time." Day took her hand and started toward the chamber where the civil ceremony was to be conducted, leaving Dulcie to follow with Beth Ann.

As they stepped inside, the judge welcomed them, then gestured to a man waiting to one side. "The photographer is waiting, Mr. Kincaid."

A photographer? Angel turned to Day, stretching on tiptoe to press a spontaneous kiss against his jaw, but at the last minute, he turned his head and caught her mouth with his own.

Her body caught fire in that special way only he could ignite and she opened her mouth to deepen the kiss. He settled his hands at her waist, pulling her even closer for a moment. "Spontaneous combustion," he said against her lips before drawing back. "Let's hold that thought for about twelve hours."

She smiled, giddy with happiness, awash with her love for him. "Gladly."

She hadn't expected to be overwhelmed by the vows. After all, she'd been married before. She knew exactly how little those solemn sentences could mean to a man. And she had no illusions about the exact nature of Day's need for her. The L-word didn't figure in there anywhere.

Still, when she spoke the phrases of commitment and heard his deep voice repeating the same words, she was moved. When he slipped the simple gold band onto her ring finger, she realized that it was already warm from his flesh. Her heart cried out in unexpected protest. This should be real.

And when he gathered her close to seal their pledges with a kiss, she responded with her entire being. If this wasn't forever, she'd make every memory count.

The entire ceremony took only minutes, not even long enough for Beth Ann to get squirmy. Afterward, the witnesses signed the marriage certificate and they posed for a few pictures with the photographer. Then Day said, "Lunchtime. I made reservations for us at—"

"Not for me," Dulcie said quickly. "I have to get back to Albuquerque."

"But you just got here," Angel protested. "You can leave right after lunch."

"Sorry." Dulcie shook her head. "I really have to get going." She embraced Angel. "Thank you for doing this," she whispered. For a moment, Angel didn't understand. With comprehension came a distinct let-down feeling. Day must have told Dulcie the circumstances surrounding this marriage. Though she couldn't fault him, the knowledge deflated her happiness as Dulcie hugged her brother with hasty but sincere congratulations, then turned to Beth Ann. "C'mon, Bethie. You can come with me out to the car."

When she and the child had moved down the hall a little way, Angel glanced at Day. He was watching his sister's back with intense concentration and she seized the chance to avoid any more personal discussion. "She seems... fragile right now."

He was still staring at his sister. "That lousy husband of hers uses her for a doormat. But she can't see it." He squared his shoulders. "And I can't seem to do anything about it. She has to manage her own life now." He offered her his arm, shaking off his concern and grinning at her. "Let's go. I have to find a drugstore before we leave town again."

"By all means, let's not forget that detail." She forced herself to smile back. She'd made this bed herself, knowing fully the realities of loving him. She couldn't complain about lying in it—even if it didn't include the love she craved.

Tonight couldn't come fast enough for him. As soon as they'd put Beth Ann to bed, he took Angel's hand and led her down the hall. Forcing himself to move slowly, he closed the bedroom door behind them and flipped on the monitor that was connected to his daughter's room. Then he turned to her.

"It seems like I've been wanting you forever," he said. She didn't speak, but her features smoothed into a soft smile in the moonlight that shone through the two windows. They had both changed into everyday clothing when they'd returned home from the wedding lunch, and he raised his hands to the snaps that ran down the front of her shirt. "May I?"

Slowly she nodded.

His mouth was dry. He was shocked to notice that his hands were trembling. When had it become so important to him to make sure this moment was perfect? True, he'd always enjoyed pleasing the women he'd bedded, but he couldn't recall worrying about it before.

But no other woman had come close to being as important to him as Angel had.

The thought halted his fingers in the act of spreading open the shirt. It was easier to concentrate on her than to confront his own feelings, so he lowered his head and touched his lips to hers, finding tenderness the only acceptable way of expressing how he was feeling.

She tilted up her face, giving him easy access, and he lingered over her features, brushing kisses over an eyebrow here, a cheekbone there, the fine, pure line of her jaw.... The voice within him quieted. He'd thought of little else all day, besides having her naked and willing beneath him.... His body was already reacting to her, stirring to life with a vibrant intensity that caused his trembling fingers to fumble over the zip of her jeans. He drew back to look at what he was doing.

Soft, pale flesh gleamed between the opened panels of her shirt. Beneath it she was wearing a black bra that emphasized the full curves it contained. Her belt hung open, and as he drew down the zipper, a tiny swatch of black panty, cut higher than could possibly be legal, sashayed into view.

His breath whistled out of his lungs. "You're so beautiful," he whispered. He slipped his hands inside her shirt, palms against the soft curve of her waist, and held her loosely. Forcing himself to take a few deep breaths, he slowly smoothed his hands up the sides of her torso, then moved them equally slowly back down again to the satiny feminine swell of her hips. His hands looked large and dark against her white skin.

Funny, he never thought of Angel as delicate, though seeing her here, now, she undoubtedly was. She had so much...*presence*. Nothing to do with her fame, but more an inner capability that he doubted she was aware she radiated. She'd helped with his household from the first day she'd been here, as if not doing so wasn't even an option. Beth Ann had warmed up to her faster than he'd ever seen his daughter take to a stranger before, and Angel obviously returned the child's affection.

At that moment, she put her hands against his cheeks, cradling his jaw. Every thought in his head went flying right out the window, along with any restraint he thought he might have.

Articles of clothing flew off in a fevered rush, discarded by fingers anxious to touch, to savor. When they both stood naked in the moonlight, he took her hand and led her to the wide bed, pulling back the covers and following her down. He stretched out on his side next to her and placed one palm low on her abdomen. "I want to be inside you."

She swallowed, turning her face toward him. "All right."

A bubble of frustrated laughter rose inside him, despite the desire raging through his system. "That was less than enthusiastic."

She managed a smile, raising her hand to stroke down his chest, though he noticed she stopped well short of any dangerous territory. "I'm sorry. I want you, too. I guess I'm just a little nervous."

"Why?" He wanted nothing more than to submerge his senses in her, to forge forward, but more than that, he wanted her to be as wild for him as he felt right now about her.

Her gaze dropped away, and even in the darkness, the loss of contact bothered him. "It's been...a long time since I had...a physical relationship with anyone."

Her admission bothered him, but not because he was afraid of hurting her. Her husky words conjured up images in his head, scenes of Angel lying with some other man as she lay with him now. How many had there been?

And what, to her, constituted a long time? Two weeks? Two months? A year?

He didn't want to know, didn't want to discuss her past. For now, he wanted to pretend that she belonged only to him. That he was the only man she'd ever known.

Dropping his head, he pressed a demanding kiss to her lips, searching, seeking out response until he found it. His hand moved in small circles across the fine skin of her belly and he lifted his mouth a fraction away from hers. "You don't have to worry. I'm going to take good care of you."

To prove his point, he kissed her again, then concentrated all his energies on arousing her. Slowly, sweetly, he touched his mouth to her throat, sliding it down the slim column onto the upper swell of her breasts, continuing on until his lips encircled an already tightly beaded nipple. One hand came up to fondle and play with the other breast until her hips began to shift restlessly back and forth. Triumph welled within him.

Keeping his mouth at her breast, he slowly smoothed his other hand down over the silken skin of her abdomen, pausing to trace the small dimple of her navel before making a steady foray below.

The tender folds of furred flesh were damp and warm; she drew in a quick, shocked breath when he stroked a gentle finger there, and turned her face into his neck. His body was screaming at him to take her, but he gritted his teeth and ignored his pounding pulse. He stroked her a second time, and she arched her heels into the mattress and gave a strangled cry.

With frantic fingers, he reached for the small package on the bedside table and covered his rigid flesh. Then, easing himself over her, he positioned himself at the humid entrance to her body. Her hips had stopped moving. Wanting to take her with him, he used his own hard length to stroke her without entering her, until her breath was coming in shallow gulps and her body was pushing up against him with every rhythmic beat.

"Please!" she whispered.

Triumph surged through him. Rearing back, he thrust forward, sheathing himself within her in a single strong stroke. Her hands and heels came up to wrap around him as her back arched again. He began to move, his whole body responding to the primal messages tingling through him. A force pressed against his spine; his body felt tense, taut, his skin too small for the flesh it contained.

Beneath him, she moaned and matched his wild riding. Suddenly her body stiffened and shook. He could feel her clasping him deep inside, her body repeating the intimate caress with a decreasing intensity that signaled release. Completely out of control, he followed her to a sweet peak of pleasure so sharp that for a few seconds it was nearly pain.

As relaxation winged through his sated body, he placed his hands at her jaw and turned her face to his for a consuming kiss.

Loving Day was both heaven and hell. It made each moment of the nights in his arms a sweet, wild memory that she stored in her heart for later.

Later. When she no longer had Day to chase away her loneliness with his lips. When Beth Ann could no longer come running, waving a picture book, expecting to be cuddled as they shared it together.

She couldn't dwell on those thoughts or she'd go mad. In the days after Emmie's adoption, she'd learned the art of acting for that very reason. She hadn't needed any courses to teach her how to put on a front, a face that wasn't hers. Pain was the best teacher there was.

She called on those skills now. Knowing how predictable the ranch routine was helped immeasurably. At night, she was Day's lover, by morning, his helpmeet. When he left the house for the day's work, she became Beth Ann's mother. Then around dinnertime, she slipped back into the role of homemaker again, becoming lover only after darkness fell and the world was silent.

Day shed his public persona only in the privacy of their bedroom, so she followed suit. Kissing, touching, holding. Those things weren't done in front of all the other people who were constantly underfoot around the ranch. Intimacies were conducted only in the dim light of the bedside lamp.

And what intimacies they were! Day was a demanding lover, calling responses from her long after she swore she had nothing left to give.

But he was also a careful lover. The cautiousness with which he always made sure she was protected saddened her, though she knew that reaction wasn't logical or even particularly rational. Deep in her heart, she longed for this relationship to be lasting. She wanted to be here always, to age with him and to see Beth Ann grow up, but more than that, she wanted to give him a child they'd made together.

The thought startled her. When she'd found out she was pregnant with Jimmy's child, she'd despaired. He was still a child himself—they hadn't been ready for parenting. And after Jimmy had died, she'd made the entirely reasonable decision to give up the baby for adoption.

Rational. Sensible. Logical. And then Emmie had been born and all her reasons had flown out the window as the love for her little miracle had blossomed. The only thing that had held her to her plans had been the knowledge that as a widowed waitress she wouldn't have had the time or the financial resources to give Emmie the love and security she deserved.

But this time it could be different. She had all the resources a woman could ever wish for, not only from her marriage but also because of the enormous success of her career.

If only her marriage wasn't temporary.

One afternoon, five days into the marriage, she was helping Beth Ann make cookie-cutter shapes with modeling clay when the telephone rang.

She walked across the kitchen to the desk. "Red Arrow Ranch."

"Is this Angelique Sumner?" It was a woman's voice, smooth and confident.

She nearly dropped the phone. Angelique Sumner! "Who is this?" she asked with cautious dread.

"Penelope Rennolt with the *Los Angeles Daily Sun*. Is this Miss Sumner speaking?"

"No." She didn't even hesitate. "You must be mistaken. This is the Red Arrow Ranch."

The reporter's low laugh scraped across her nerves. "I don't think there's any mistake. Angelique Sumner Vandervere married New Mexico rancher, David Kincaid, a few days ago. Kincaid, who just happens to be the less-than-amicable ex-husband of Jada Barrington, owns the Red Arrow Ranch. So where else would he have stashed his blushing bride? Any comment? Is a honeymoon in the offing?"

Angel slammed down the phone so sharply that Beth Ann looked up with a frown. "Daddy does that when he talks to my other mommy," she informed Angel. "Were you talking to Mommy?"

It was an effort to smile, to paste a natural expression on her face, when all she wanted to do was scream and yell and throw things. "No, honey," she forced herself to say in a soft tone. "It wasn't your mommy." She walked back to the table and sat down. "Okay. We need to start cleaning up so we have time to read a story before nap time."

She paced and puzzled the whole time the child slept. How had they found her? Had someone recognized her at the dance in Deming?

After Beth Ann awoke, Angel saddled the pretty mare Day had given her to ride, set the child before her in the saddle and rode out to get the mail. It would have been faster and easier to take the truck, but she needed something—anything—to occupy her until time to begin the dinner preparations. Beth Ann loved horseback rides and all her young energies were taken up with pretending she was guiding the mare, racing across the desert, zipping through the barrel-race event at the rodeo or roping a bawling calf. All Angel's energies were occupied with keeping her on the horse.

When they reached the mailbox, Angel leaned down to pluck the mail and the newspaper from the roadside boxes. Mindful of Day's warnings about Old Red, who was eyeing them from several hundred feet away, she stayed in the saddle with Beth Ann. Riding back to the barn, she was surprised to see Day's horse in its stall.

After she'd put the mare away and cleaned up her tack, she walked slowly toward the house. Day was going to be madder than that old bull on a rampage when he learned that her movie persona had followed her here.

Walking into the house, she saw him leaning against the counter. His expression was unsmiling and her heart sank.

He knew.

How could he?

Beth Ann went skipping to him, reaching up in an unspoken plea to be lifted into his arms, and the darkness in his gaze vanished. "Hey, filly. What have you been up to?"

The little girl snuggled against him, chubby fingers toying with the snaps on the front of his shirt. "Me an' Ang— Mommy took a ride out to the mailbox." She drew back and stared earnestly into his eyes. "Daddy, when am I gonna be old enough for my own pony?"

Day grinned and lightly kissed the end of his daughter's nose. "Soon. I guess you're getting big enough to start learning how to sit a horse." He set the child on the floor. "Want to watch your favorite shows until dinner?"

"Yeah!" Beth Ann wasn't permitted to watch much television and she happily scampered into the living room and settled herself on the couch while Day turned to a popular children's show.

In a moment, he returned to the kitchen. "We have to talk."

"I know." Puzzlement colored her tone. "You already know that our marriage has been leaked to the press? That somebody figured out who I am?"

"Yeah. The phone rang awhile ago while I was in the barn. When nobody picked it up at the house, I grabbed it." He scowled and she cringed inwardly.

"I'm sorry." She shrugged helplessly. "I don't know how they found—"

The ringing of the telephone cut off her words.

Day snatched up the receiver. "Red Arrow Ranch." He listened for a few seconds, then slammed the instrument back into its cradle. She could see him practically snarling. "Another one."

Before she could say anything, they heard the cough of an unfamiliar engine as it ground to a halt before the house. Day's eyebrows rose, then he was striding to the front door.

Angel was right behind him. When Day opened the door, she got a good look at a shaggy-haired young man loaded with camera equipment coming across the dusty yard. Shoving her back into the house, Day muttered, "Stay out of sight."

Stay out of sight! She instantly rebelled at the autocratic male tone, but a moment later she had to admit that he was smart. The last thing Day needed were photos of her at his ranch to confirm the stories. Racing into his office, which looked out over the front of the house, she peeked through the blinds.

The guy with the cameras was being herded steadily toward his car. Day appeared to be doing all the talking, a forceful finger stabbing repeatedly into the guy's chest, sending him stumbling back a pace at a time.

As he pushed the man into his car, two of the ranch hands came riding up. Day gave them some terse instructions in a voice too low for her straining ears to hear and they wheeled toward the barn. The small car bumped down the road away from the house and then she saw the two hands on horseback setting out in the same direction. Across their saddles lay rifles.

Frantically she bolted out onto the porch. "Are you crazy?" she shouted at Day.

"If I wasn't," he said, taking the steps two at a time to stand beside her on the porch, "this will do it."

"You can't just let them shoot people! Why did—"

"Whoa, hold on." Day grasped her by the shoulders and gave her a gentle shake. "They aren't going to shoot anybody. They're just escorting a trespasser off our land and making sure anybody else who's aiming to try it thinks twice."

His voice was tolerant and mildly amused, but she saw the black remains of rage in his eyes. He must have been livid to hear that news of their marriage had gotten out. Privacy was important to him, more so because of Beth Ann and who her mother was.

Guilt rose. It was her fault. She should have known this wouldn't work. She still hadn't figured out how the press had learned of her location, but she hadn't been exactly hiding. A diligent digger getting a few lucky breaks could have done it.

As they reentered the house, the telephone rang.

If Day's expression could grow any blacker, she couldn't imagine how. He snatched up the phone and barked, "What?" Then he held out the receiver to her. "Karl Graines. He says he's your agent."

She took the instrument as if it were poisonous. "Hello?"

"Angelique, how could you have done this to me? The press is hounding me for details about your wedding and I didn't even know about it!" A melodramatic baritone rolled across the wires.

She smiled despite herself, twining the phone cord around one finger. "Hello, Karl."

He steamrolled right over her greeting. "Oh, darling. How could you have done this?"

"Done what?"

"This... this marriage. Without confiding in me. As if it isn't bad enough that you've been out of touch for ages—"

"Only a few weeks," she interrupted. "And you had my number for emergencies. You know good and well I needed the rest."

"Rest? You've obviously been doing more than resting," he said. When she made no comment, he went on. "Yes, well, now that you're rested, I have a couple of things I'd like you to look at and—"

"No." Her response cut short enough to make Day's eyebrows rise. "I told you I'm not sure I want to take on anything else."

"But, darling, these are good. One in particular would be perfect. Just let me send them down and you can take a quick glance. I got one yesterday that looks simply divine...."

But she wasn't listening. Day had reached into the cupboard and pulled out a glass, which he'd filled with cold water. He lifted the glass to his lips, and the smooth muscles in his tanned throat worked as he drained the contents. When he set the glass in the sink, she saw that his lips were wet and gleaming, and instantly her mind went winging back to those dark, sweet hours in the night, hours when he set those lips on her body and played her like a finely tuned instrument until not another note would come.

What would she do without him? He'd made no pretense. Right from the start, she'd known her time as his wife would be limited. Maybe she should read the scripts, she thought with weary resignation. True, she didn't want to go back to the public life she'd led, but if she couldn't be with Day, what did it matter? There were going to be a lot of empty hours in her days. Too empty. She had to make plans to do something; it might as well be another role.

"I don't know," she said to Karl, her gaze still on the man before her. "Send the scripts to me. If I get a chance, I'll look them over."

Day's head came up sharply at the last sentence. His eyes narrowed as he stared at her, saw the helpless attraction she couldn't hide.

As she gave Karl the ranch's address and rang off, Day crossed the kitchen. She barely had time to set down the receiver before he was pulling her into his arms, kissing her without finesse but with a deep, aching hunger that made her toes curl and her body sag against him.

It was the first time since they had married that he'd shown his desire for her in the middle of the day like this, and when he lifted her to the counter and moved between her legs, she didn't even think to protest. He explored her breasts through her soft cotton shirt, his fingers moving until her nipples were hard peaks. . . .

The telephone rang again.

There was bad timing and then there was *bad timing*.

Reluctantly releasing Angel, Day stepped away from her and lifted the receiver. The way he felt right now, whoever was on the other end should be glad they weren't within reach. He was going to call the phone company as soon as he'd dealt with this and have the damned number changed.

"This better be good," he barked.

The silence on the other end of the line was exactly what he'd expected. But when his ex-wife's shrill voice demanded, "Day? Is that you?" he let out his breath in a frustrated groan.

Hell. The last thing he needed right now was another unproductive argument with the woman who—unfortunately—was the mother of his child.

With the same wary caution he reserved for sidewinders and scorpions, he said, "It's me, Jada." Out of the corner of his eye, he saw Angel's involuntary movement, but as she turned to leave he pointed to the stool at the counter. "Sit," he mouthed.

Jada's voice grated in his ear. "You think you're pretty smart, don't you? You think that just because you have a wife now you're going to hoodwink some local judge into awarding you custody of *my* daughter." The venom in her voice was unmistakable.

"She's my daughter, too," he said through gritted teeth.

"I don't care!" Her voice rose, high and sharp and hateful. "Do you think that bringing a slut like Sumner into your house is actually going to *help* your case? Let me tell you, I've heard things about that woman that make my hair curl. How you could allow a woman with her reputation—"

Fury bit at him. He tamped it down and forced mockery into his voice. "It's amazing to me that you, of all people, would be concerned about somebody else's reputation." Then the rage that fanned his temper tested its bonds and broke free. "Let me tell you something, Jada. Angel has more integrity than you can even imagine. Her soul isn't rotten like yours."

As the words echoed down the wire, he realized they were true. Jada could have been a postal worker, a computer operator or a doctor, and she still wouldn't be a decent person. The rot that ate away at her went too deep to excise.

She was nothing like Angel. Other than a superficial connection through similar careers, the two women were opposites in every way there was.

And Angel was the one he wanted.

"Just keep pushing me," he warned Jada. "You want to keep playing games? Try this one. If I get one more phone call, you try one more legal maneuver stalling my bid for custody, I'm going to the papers. I'm sure they'll be more than mildly interested in my version of your Lady Bountiful act. Your child cries when she thinks you're going to take her back. She's terrified of the dark and of getting dirty or making noise. She once begged me not to make her sit in the closet. You want to explain that to the press? Come to think of it, maybe I'll just let them talk to Beth Ann herself."

"You wouldn't." Her voice was low and furious.

She was right. He wouldn't. Not out of any concern for Jada, but because he loved his child. He refused to allow Beth Ann to be traumatized any further. But Jada had no such scruples, and she would believe any threats he made.

"Just watch and see," he promised. "If I don't have signed custody papers in my hands within seven days, I go to the press."

He had to hold the phone away from his ear at the vituperative eruption of filthy language that next spewed out of her mouth. "You son of a bitch—I'll ruin you!" she screamed. "I'll make you sorry—"

He set down the receiver, cutting her off.

Angel was still sitting on the stool. Her eyes were huge and he realized Jada had been loud enough for her to hear most of the exchange for herself.

"I wouldn't really put Beth Ann through that," he began.

She waved a hand impatiently. "I know that. But she doesn't, and if it helps, it will have been worth it." Her face grew thoughtful. "I thought maybe you were wrong, you know," she said, addressing the top of the counter rather than meeting his gaze. "I just couldn't imagine that anyone could resist that sweet little girl—" Her voice broke, then firmed again. "I don't want to take any chances that might cost you your daughter. I couldn't bear it if Beth Ann ever went back to that woman. If my presence here is going to cause problems—"

"No." He took her hands and she looked up at him for the first time. Her eyes were so full of pain he could hardly bear it, and he wondered what she was thinking of. "I married you because you can help me keep my daughter. Don't worry about Jada. As for what you thought—Jada doesn't love anyone except herself. When Beth Ann was a baby, she was too much trouble—Jada couldn't be bothered. Now that she's a little older, Jada sees a publicity opportunity. And the reverse is true, too. Losing custody of her child won't look good."

"Why don't you have your lawyer suggest to hers that you're willing to be very quiet about the custody thing?" Angel looked thoughtfully at their joined hands. "Maybe even plant the idea that Jada is giving up custody voluntarily in Beth Ann's best interests, because she's concerned about her growing up in the Hollywood environment."

What a woman! He was already nodding in agreement as he dropped her hands and reached for the phone. "Great idea. I'll make the call right now."

Beth Ann took a late nap the following day. Angel was afraid of photo hounds near the main road, so she asked one of the hands to ride out to pick up the mail. Since Day had turned on the answering machine, the house had been blessedly quiet. By late last evening, Day had unplugged the phones to prevent any more reporters from intruding into their lives.

She smiled to herself as she mixed the filling for cherry pies. Over and over again, she heard Day telling Jada that she had integrity. Finally he had recognized that she wasn't just like Jada simply because they shared a common profession.

The porch door banged and she looked up with a smile, hoping it was Day, but it was only Smokey coming back with the mail. The redheaded cowboy brought it in and laid it on the kitchen counter, drooled over the pie filling and beat a hasty retreat when she flicked a dish towel at him.

Distracted by the crust she was making, which was turning out to be tougher than she'd expected to work with, Angel didn't glance through the stack until just before dinner.

A large overnight package caught her eye first. She already knew what it was. Scripts. Karl had been as prompt as he'd promised. She felt like reading them as much as— as she did leaving the Red Arrow. Idly she glanced through the rest of the mail. Mostly bills for Day.

It was the third envelope from the bottom.

She felt the shock slam into her, felt herself sway as she recognized the familiar envelope. Deep breath. Take a deep breath.

She did. Groping for the nearest chair, she sagged into it. Dear God, she'd thought that whoever had been writing these had forgotten her.

She'd *wanted* to forget, that was for sure. The ranch had been a haven, a new beginning, and she'd been so positive that she wasn't interesting enough to merit this obsession outlasting her disappearance.

She'd been wrong. Whoever was—was *stalking* her must be crazy. Really crazy. Not just a little nutty like some of her fans. The sounds of trucks and men coming into the yard galvanized her into action. Taking the letter from the stack, she sprinted up the stairs to the bedroom she now shared with Day.

She couldn't worry him with this. Not now, when he was already half-crazed by the changes her presence had made in his life. Threats from his ex-wife, a custody suit, the loss of the privacy he so valued . . . no, she couldn't. She'd just send it to the L.A. police like she had all the others.

Carefully she opened the envelope and slid out the single sheet of paper with a letter opener. Unfolding it with the same instrument, she studied the short message it contained as if she could learn something from it.

I can't wait to see you again.

She shuddered. Even here, she wasn't safe. She wondered how he'd gotten her address. It didn't matter, because now he knew where to find her.

She slipped the letter into her lingerie drawer, but as she prepared to close the drawer, the postmark on the envelope caught her eye.

Deming.

Nine

Angel had been different ever since those damned scripts had arrived. Day had noticed at dinner that she'd seemed subdued, upset about something. Later, when they were watching television together, she'd opened a package she'd apparently received with the day's mail. He'd seen scripts when Jada had lived with him, so he knew instantly what these were.

But she never mentioned them. Was she thinking of accepting another role? Making another movie? Dissatisfaction tore through him and he ruthlessly squashed it. He'd known when he asked her to marry him that it would be temporary, that a woman like her didn't belong here on the ranch.

Was she sorry she'd married him? He was positive she genuinely loved Beth Ann. And heaven knew, the passion that flared between them every night wasn't a problem. Unless you counted the fact that neither one of them was getting enough sleep because they couldn't keep their hands off each other.

Still . . . the danger from whoever had been stalking her appeared to have vanished. Even though her name and location had been splashed all over the news for the past few days, there had been no contact, no threats of any kind. The guy had probably fixated on some other unlucky woman by now.

She'd said she didn't want to return to an acting career. Still . . . it looked to him as if that's exactly where she was headed. With as little delay as possible.

Well, it was no skin off his nose. With any luck, he would soon have custody of Beth Ann, which was the only reason he'd married her.

Soon he wouldn't need her anymore.

Of course he wouldn't.

"Day?"

Her voice intruded into his dark thoughts. How long had she been trying to get his attention? "Sorry," he said, mentally filing away all thoughts of her leaving. She was here now, and he might as well take full advantage of it.

He got up out of the recliner he'd been sitting in and moved to sit beside her on the couch. She'd laid her package aside, and when he looped an arm around her and pulled her onto his chest, she lifted her face to his and they shared a slow, deep kiss.

When he raised his head, his voice was hoarse and his body was throbbing. No woman had ever been able to make him so hot with only a single kiss. "Let's go to bed." It wasn't a suggestion.

To his surprise, she drew back a little. "Can we talk for a few minutes first?"

Talk was the last thing on his mind. He gave himself an approving pat on the back for being able to say, "Sure," without a trace of disgruntled male irritation. "What's on your mind?" He tensed as it occurred to him that what she might want to discuss was a date for her to leave, if he got the custody papers as expected.

"Beth Ann."

He relaxed again.

"I think it's a mistake to allow her to carry her blanket everywhere with her."

It was the last thing he'd expected her to say. He felt his hackles rise automatically and he tried to hide it. "I don't think it's a big deal."

"It is when she sucks her thumb every time she touches it. I've noticed that she doesn't suck her thumb at all unless she has her blanket."

Reaching for patience, he said, "When I got her home from her last visit to Jada, that blanket was the only thing that comforted her. If it makes her feel secure, why upset her by taking it away?"

"If I thought she really needed it for emotional comfort, I'd agree." Angel was sitting up now, turned toward him. Her eyes glowed with the intensity of her words. "But I think it's just a habit now, one that needs to be eliminated, at least during the day, before her teeth are damaged by the constant thumb-sucking."

"That's an old wives' tale." He had no idea, but he wasn't about to let her get the upper hand.

"No, it isn't. I called a dentist in Las Cruces yesterday, and he said that continued thumb-sucking could change the shape of her palate, leading to problems later that might require braces."

"So we get braces if she needs them." He shrugged, more because he didn't want her to know she was right than because he disagreed. Actually, her words concerned him. And shamed him. Beth Ann was his responsibility. He should have thought of it himself.

"I really don't think she needs it to make her feel secure anymore, except, of course, during the night," she said again. "Why are you being so stubborn?"

"Why are you so concerned about it?" he countered. Defensiveness made his tone sharp. "Who made you the authority on child rearing? You've never even been a parent."

As soon as he said it, he regretted the cheap shot. Then alarm replaced regret as color leached from her cheeks with a dramatic suddenness that he wouldn't have believed if he hadn't seen it.

She wrapped her arms around herself as if she was chilled and her head bowed until all he could see was the crown of her shining blond hair. "You're wrong." Her words were barely audible and he had to lean forward to hear her. "I was a parent once. But I gave my baby away when she was two months old." Her voice wavered and cracked on the last words. She began to rock back and forth, caught in a past too painful for him to share.

He sagged back against the cushions, stunned by her words. "When?"

She made a strangled sound and bolted off the couch.

Too late, he realized his reaction had been insensitive, thoughtless. But dammit, she'd shocked the socks off him.

"Angel! Sweetheart, wait." He reached for her but she shrugged off his hand. "We have to talk about this."

"I c-can't." She backed away, flinching when he rose to his feet. "I'm tired. I need to go to bed."

The bone-deep weariness and sorrow in her whispered voice cut him to the quick. He knew, without being a brain surgeon, that she wouldn't be sleeping in his bed tonight, but he also knew, without a hint of doubt, that if he pressured her, she'd leave.

And that was the last thing he wanted.

Day didn't have time to talk to Angel in the morning and she carefully avoided his gaze while she prepared breakfast and lunches. But when it came time for him to walk out to the barn, he found that he couldn't go off without trying to fix things between them.

As the last of the hands clumped out of the house, he caught her by the hand and drew her to him. He perched on a stool at the counter, placing her between his knees. Reaching for her other hand, he rubbed his thumbs back and forth across her knuckles, trying to figure out how to phrase what he wanted to say.

Finally, all he said was "I'm sorry."

Her eyes filled with tears and her lower lip trembled; she bit down fiercely on it as he pulled her into his arms and began to rub her back. She was as stiff as a fence post in his grasp.

At last she drew away a little and said, "Thank you."

He didn't remove his arms completely, though he could tell she was itching to get loose and flee the room. "I didn't mean to act like a such a jerk last night," he said, gazing straight into her eyes. "I was . . . surprised. Tonight, will you tell me about it? About your baby?"

She nodded, still worrying her lip between her teeth. A single tear slipped down her cheek.

He caught it with his thumb, then brushed a gentle finger over her lip. "Cut it out before you hurt yourself." He pulled her close again, not even wanting to kiss her so much as simply to comfort her, and this time she let him rock her in his embrace until the rigidity left her body and she was limp against him. The sound of a horse leaving the yard reminded him of the work that wouldn't wait and he had to force himself to set her away from him, gently kissing her temple. "I'll see you later."

In midafternoon, the gelding he was riding to cull cows from the herd threw a shoe and went lame. He loaded the cutter into one of the stock trailers they used to haul the cows they were going to sell, then drove back to the barn, where he worked over the injured horse's leg. When he pared down the foot, he uncovered an abscess that was brewing, so he cleaned it out and let it begin to drain.

Finishing up, he went into the saddle room to wash the blood from his hands. Then he called the vet to get some antibiotics for the gelding. The sound of a motor interrupted him just as he was deliberating whether or not it was too late to take another horse and rejoin the men. He walked to the barn door and leaned against the frame.

To his astonishment, the vehicle bumping toward the house was a florist's delivery van from Deming. He stepped out of the shadow of the barn and waved his hand, and the driver detoured toward him.

"Mighty far out of town," he said as the man rolled down his window.

"Don't I know it. But some fool paid three times the price to have these flowers hand delivered to the Red Arrow Ranch." The guy eyed him quizzically. "It true that Angelique Sumner married the cowboy who owns this spread?"

Day jerked his head forward briefly at the stranger. The guy obviously didn't take him for the "cowboy who owns this spread." "Yep."

The man whistled. "Whoo-eee! Bet I wouldn't like to get next to her! You seen her?"

Day shrugged, his temper thinning. "Not much." He looked pointedly at the back of the van. "You got a delivery, give it here, and I'll take it on up to the house."

The man's face fell and it would have been comical if jealousy and irritation hadn't eaten Day's sense of humor down to a nub. "I don't mind. I was hoping she'd answer the door."

"You aren't going to get near her." He knew his voice had been too harsh when the man cast him a speculative glance, but at least the driver got out of the van and hurried around to the side door.

"All right, then, I'll give 'em to you."

Jealousy turned to outright rage when the man pulled an enormous spray of bloodred roses from the van and deposited them in his arms with a brief spate of instructions on their care. As the vehicle trundled away in the direction of the main road, he stalked toward the house with the damned flowers.

A white envelope tucked in among the blossoms tantalized him. He was tempted to forget his good manners and read it but his hands were too full.

Angel met him at the door. "I heard somebody coming as I was putting Beth Ann down for her nap— Oh!" Her face melted into lines of pleased happiness. "These are beautiful. Thank you."

As he set the heavy vase on the kitchen counter, she moved toward him but he forestalled her. "They're not from me."

Her smile dimmed to uncertainty, which then shaded into bewilderment. "They're not?"

Oh, she was good. Of all the women in the world, he had to get involved with another actress. "No," he said grimly, "they're not. I just happened to meet the delivery van."

"Then who...?" A frown made small parallel furrows of puzzlement between her brows. She turned to the bouquet and detached the little white envelope.

He folded his arms and stood waiting as she pulled a small card out and read the message. His face felt stiff with anger; he wanted to tear the card from her hands and shred it into tiny pieces. She was his, dammit! And nobody else was going to—

Angel made a small sound and swayed.

What the hell! He grabbed for her as her knees buckled, barely catching her in time to keep her from slumping to the floor. The card she'd dropped fluttered down a foot away and he reached for it, wondering what could be so terrible that it could make her faint.

Soon we'll be together again.

No signature. He didn't get it. But before he could puzzle any longer, Angel's limp body began to struggle in his arms. He set her upright though he kept his arms around her in case she passed out again. Her face was chalk white and she shuddered when she saw the note he held in his hand.

"Oh, God..."

Was she afraid he was going to be angry? His ire returned with a rush. He damned well had a right to be. She'd deliberately led him to believe that she wasn't involved with anyone, that she was as pure as the driven snow.

Releasing her, he extended the card to her. She reacted violently, trying to scramble backward away from it. "No!"

He looked at the card, then at her. She was acting like... like she was terrified of the card. If he'd had a free hand, he'd have smacked himself in the forehead as the truth dawned. She didn't have a man stashed somewhere.

The flowers were from whoever was stalking her.

"They're from him."

Angel nodded, knowing what Day meant without further discussion. He had replaced the card in the bouquet of roses, and she looked at it, loathing and fear rising in equal proportions. "Get rid of them," she said. Her voice sounded shaky and weak, not strong and commanding as she'd intended.

Day extended a hand to pull her to her feet. "You got it. And then you're going to tell me all about this." He grabbed the vase and shouldered the back door open; she heard a crash as he unceremoniously dumped the hateful flowers into a large trash can.

She poured each of them a large glass of iced tea and perched at the counter. When he came back in, he tipped back his head and drained the glass before setting it down with a loud sigh.

"Okay," he said. "What makes you think this guy—this stalker—sent you the roses?" When she hesitated, he turned and moved closer in until his face was bare inches from hers. "I can't help you if you don't trust me," he said through his teeth.

It was exactly what she needed to take her mind off her peril and defeat the last remnants of fear. "Why should I trust you?" she countered. "You don't trust me. Despite everything I've told you to the contrary, you believed those flowers were from another man." She linked her fingers together and stared at them, afraid of revealing too much.

"I haven't lied to you about other men, Day."

"I know." His voice was low. A dull flush crept up his neck to bronze his tanned cheeks. "It was easier to think you couldn't be trusted than to let you get under my skin."

"Have I gotten under your skin?" She held her breath, hoping against hope for some small sign—anything!—to indicate that she meant something more to him than simply a warm body that was exclusively his for the time being.

"Have you ever." Swiveling his stool to face hers, he placed his hands on her knees and moved them apart, pressing himself against her. "I can't stand the thought of anyone else touching you," he said roughly. "Thinking about you with some other fella had me so irritated I could hardly see straight."

It wasn't what she'd been looking for, but it was a start. If his desire for her was that strong, if it was lasting, perhaps it would make the transition into love one day. "I don't want to be touched by anyone but you," she whispered. "Only you, Day."

He kissed her then and she curled into him, wordlessly giving him everything she couldn't say. When he lifted his head, his eyes were glittering with arousal and he was breathing heavily. She lifted a finger to the hard length of man behind the zipper of his worn jeans and rubbed gently against him. He groaned. "Unless you're planning on finishing what you started, you'd better get your hands out of there."

She smiled up at him without moving her hand. "Beth Ann will be awake soon."

Lifting her hand away, he bared his teeth in a smile. "Tease. Just wait 'til tonight." Then the laughter died from his face as he stepped away from her. "You've managed to completely sidetrack me, haven't you? I still want to know what made you so sure the flowers came from the same guy who sent you the letters in L.A. I thought he'd forgotten about you after you dropped out of sight."

"So did I." She gave a resigned sigh. "I felt so safe for a while. I almost forgot to be afraid. But the moment the news came out about our marriage and where I was living, he sent me another letter."

His head came up sharply and he stared at her until she dropped her gaze from his. "And you didn't think I'd want to know? Dammit, Angel, what were you thinking?"

She swallowed. "I—it was my problem, not yours. You've had enough to worry about."

"Hey." He waited until she was looking at him once again. "It's our problem. You're my wife, remember?" When she nodded, he went on. "I want to see the letter."

"Now?"

"Now."

Wordlessly she got to her feet and left the room to return a moment later holding an envelope gingerly by one corner. She dropped it in his lap and took a seat at the far end of the couch as he stared at the innocent-looking pieces of paper.

When he lifted his head, his gaze speared hers with angry incredulity. "It's postmarked from Deming."

* * *

The sheriff came out right after dinner. At Day's request, he had contacted the police in L.A. to whom Angel had reported the other letters and messages she'd received.

"The flowers are a dead end," the law enforcement officer said. "Ordered by phone, paid for with an envelope of cash that appeared on the counter when the cashier went into the back for a minute." The stocky man in the tan uniform shook his head ruefully. "Whoever's doing this is a careful planner." He looked at Angel, standing on the porch with her arms wrapped around herself, then at the letter in a plastic bag that he was taking with him. "He writes as if he knows you. It could be the delusion of a sick mind, or it could be he's someone from your past, possibly even someone you know now. Give it some thought and let me know if anyone, no matter how slight the connection, comes to mind."

"I'm having a tap put on the phones, too," Day told her. "If he tries to call you here like he did before, maybe we can get him that way."

"One way or the other," the sheriff said, "we'll get him." He settled his hat on his head and turned toward the patrol car. "I'll be in touch. You do the same if anything comes up."

What could come up? She shivered. Somewhere out there, somewhere *close by,* someone was waiting for her. She could almost feel his presence.

Day was determined that Angel wasn't going to sleep away from him another night. When he took her hand and led her up the steps at bedtime, he expected some initial resistance. But she followed along with an absent docility that told him more clearly than words how disturbed she was. The delivery of those flowers today had sliced into the fragile links of understanding he'd been trying to forge and disrupted all semblance of normalcy. In fact, she seemed to have forgotten all about the revelations of the night before.

Well, she might not be thinking about them, but he was. It was damn near all he'd thought about the whole day on the range...at least until he'd come in and waylaid that florist's van.

He was ready for bed before she was, and he propped himself against the pillows where he could watch her moving around the room, performing all those little feminine tasks that seemed such a part of her. She unbound her hair and brushed it out, then reached for a bottle of lotion and smoothed it down her legs, over her arms and up the slender column of her neck, her long, graceful fingers gently rubbing until her skin glowed with moisture.

He couldn't help grinning with pure pleasure as his body began to react to the sight. She didn't notice his interest as she removed the lightweight robe from her shoulders and hung it on the bedpost, then slipped between the sheets on her side of the big bed he'd shared with her since their wedding.

Being married took work, he reflected, but it had some fringe benefits he'd forgotten. Or more likely, had never known the first time around. And he wasn't just thinking of the sex, either, great as it was. Having someone to greet him at the door with a special smile meant only for him was one of those intangibles he'd never thought would be so important. Even the simple act of sharing the load, working through problems together, was nice. It created a closeness that he was slowly beginning to realize he enjoyed, valued, *needed*.

He scrunched down on his mound of pillows and slid an arm around her, drawing her in to his side. For an instant she tensed. Then she heaved an immense sigh and her body went boneless.

They lay that way in silence for a few minutes; he idly rubbed his fingertips back and forth against the silky skin of her upper arm, reveling in the sweet warmth of her cuddled against his side. He knew that the moment he brought up her past—her baby—she would withdraw faster than a threatened prairie dog, but reluctant though he was to cause her pain, he needed to know, to hear, her story from her.

Quietly he said, "We had a big day today."

"Uh-huh." Her agreement was drowsy.

"It, uh, kind of distracted me from thinking about what you told me last night." He'd been expecting her reaction and he quelled her immediate, brief struggle to pull away. "But I'd really like to hear what happened."

She had stopped trying to get away from him, but her voice was as tense as her body. "There's not much to tell. I gave you the big picture last night."

"No." He did his best to keep his voice level, quiet and soothing. "You gave me the bare bones last night. Tonight I want the details, the feelings." He paused, searching for the right words. "I know you love children. And I know you wouldn't have made such a drastic decision without carefully weighing all the options. It must have been very painful for you."

She was silent. Her body felt as taut as a guy wire, almost radiating nervous energy. Just when he was nearly convinced she wasn't going to talk to him, she sighed, a long, quivering ragged exhalation that hitched several times as she fought for control.

"I have a daughter," she said. "She'll be six years old in February. And she was adopted six years ago in April by a couple who could offer her far more than I could have at that time."

He stroked her arm with a touch designed to comfort. "Your husband died before she was born?"

She nodded. "I was five months pregnant when he died. But we'd been separated for half that—since he found out about the baby." She shrugged. "We met shortly after my high school graduation and got married a month later. Looking back, it's easy to see how desperate I was for someone of my own, someone to belong to. My parents were both dead. I was very conscious of being alone."

He couldn't imagine how she must have felt. "It must have been a frightening feeling."

"I thought getting married would change my loneliness, that finally I'd have someone to share my life with. Perhaps, with the right person, I'd have found that. But at the ripe old age of eighteen, it was too easy to confuse sex with love." She sighed. "Jimmy needed a mother, not a wife. But I didn't realize that until after the wedding. After a year, I knew it was a mistake. And when he found out I was pregnant, he couldn't make tracks in the other direction fast enough."

"And then he died."

Her eyes were open, trained on the ceiling, and he sensed that although she still lay in the circle of his arms, she was miles away. "Yes." She paused. "He crashed his pickup after a drinking spree one night."

He swallowed convulsively and clutched her to him, remembering that she'd lost her father to a violent death only a few years before she'd lost her husband.

She let him hold her, but after a moment she raised her head and one hand lifted and fell in a gesture of futility. "I was a high school graduate with no skills to speak of. But I wanted my baby. It took me a long time to acknowledge that keeping her would be nothing but an act of selfishness on my part, that I could barely afford to feed myself, much less provide for a child."

She turned and sought his gaze. "Children are the most precious gift in the world. They deserve the best that we can give them. Even before she was born, I knew I couldn't

give my child what she needed to grow up healthy and secure. So when she was a little less than two months old, a
couple from Tucson adopted her.''

Tears were running down her cheeks and her voice was
ragged. ''I'll never forget tying her little bonnet for the last
time, nursing her and holding that sweet little bundle in my
arms before I handed her to her new mother. She had just
started smiling and she smiled at me.''

Angel's pain was more than he could take. But she
wasn't finished and she waved him away when he tried to
embrace her again.

''I named her Emily, after my mother, but I called her
Emmie.'' She stopped and closed her eyes, then opened
them and went on. ''The O'Briens, her adoptive parents,
promised never to change her name. They love her dearly.
Once a year I receive a progress report and pictures from
them.'' She sniffed and attempted a smile. ''Then I cry for
a week. It's a little bit of comfort to know that Emmie is a
happy, well-adjusted child, that I made the right decision.''

''Will she—Emmie—ever be able to get in touch with
you when she's grown?'' His mind was working fever-
ishly. Surely there had to be a way to relieve some of her
anguish.

''It will be up to Emmie to decide if she wants to contact me. I wrote her a letter that she'll receive on her
twenty-first birthday. Every year I send Mrs. O'Brien a
new one to add to it. She'll read them all one day and
maybe she'll see how much I loved her.'' She stopped, and
he was thankful for her catharsis, for the chance to better
understand her, to feel what she was feeling.

Then she went on, her tone heavy with bitter irony. ''To
forget, I took acting classes and worked my fingers to the
bone waitressing. The only way I could sleep was if I was
totally exhausted, and when I woke up, I had to get out of
my apartment and be busy, or I'd have gone crazy. I didn't

give myself time to think, to feel. Two years later, I got my big break." She sent him a tremulous smile. "And now I have to live with the knowledge that giving up Emmie enabled me to become the sort of success that most people only dream of. I have enough money now to raise a dozen children." Softly she added, "And I'd give it all away tomorrow, along with the fame and recognition, if it meant I could somehow go back in time, relive the years I've lost with my child."

She made it sound so black and white, as if there weren't shades of gray that she hadn't considered. He couldn't resist asking, "Have you ever thought about trying to get Emmie back? Or at least get visitation rights?"

She smiled sadly. "Every day. I've already missed so much. But it wouldn't be fair to her or to her adoptive parents. All rights I had ended the day she was adopted, and if I tried to become part of her life now I could do more damage than good. A child's world needs to be stable and secure."

He could see the wisdom of her words, and he could only marvel at her strength. He doubted he could be so unselfish if they were talking about Beth Ann. At the same time, he became aware of how upsetting this discussion must be for her.

Abruptly he knew he'd heard enough. Anything more she wanted him to know, she could tell him in her own good time. He wasn't going to pressure her a minute more.

Quietly he drew her fully into his arms. "You're going to be exhausted tomorrow. Let's get some sleep."

She twisted like an energetic calf in his arms, so fast that before he knew it she was lying sprawled atop him. "I'm not as tired as you think." She nudged his legs wider by nestling one leg between them, rubbing lightly against him with her angled knee. Under her teasing ministrations, his soft relaxation disappeared, replaced by a steady pulsing that brought full, leaping life with every heartbeat.

In an instant, he was wildly aroused. As she dropped her head and sought his mouth, he rolled her beneath him, kissing her with hot, frantic intent, settling himself between her legs and pulling handfuls of her lacy nightie out of his way. "Is that an offer?"

She laughed, a husky, inviting sound that raced along his nerve endings as she twined her arms around his neck and urged him closer. "Are you looking for one, cowboy?"

Ten

Angel felt closer to Day than she'd ever felt before. Sharing her past with him had brought them together as nothing else could have. He had acted as if he cared. Did he? Could he? Did she dare allow herself to imagine that he might love her, that he might ask her to stay with him forever?

Three days passed, days in which she pretended that nothing was wrong with the picture-perfect moments of life on the ranch, that she wasn't being threatened by some unknown evil, that her time to be Day's wife and Beth Ann's mother wasn't limited.

About ten minutes after Day left the house one morning, the telephone rang. Startled, wondering who would be calling at such an early hour, Angel sprinted to pick up the receiver before the ringing woke Beth Ann. "Red Arrow Ranch," she greeted the caller.

No one spoke.

"Hello? May I help you?" The only reason she could imagine someone calling so early was if there was a problem, an emergency at a neighboring spread. Or maybe it was Dulcie. . . .

"Angelique." It was a masculine voice, deep and distinct.

Instant recognition streaked through her. Her idyll had ended. "Who is this?" she demanded, making her voice as firm as she could.

"You know." The man's voice was definitely familiar.

Her stomach muscles quivered—she'd heard that voice before, though not so clearly. Again she forced herself to speak in a calm, polite tone. If she could keep him on the line long enough, maybe the sheriff would be able to have the call traced. "I'm sorry, I don't recognize your voice. Who's speaking, please?"

"You know me!" The caller's voice lost a little of its smooth suavity. He sounded irritated, agitated. Then, with chilling ease, his tone became confident again. "Soon we'll be able to talk face-to-face. I've missed you, Angelique."

She was silent. How was she supposed to respond to this madman?

"Did you hear me?" He sounded angry again.

All of a sudden she'd had enough. Enough of looking over her shoulder all the time, enough of staring at the ceiling in the dark sweating out every unusual noise. Enough! "I don't know who you are and I don't really care," she said, intense rage at this unwarranted invasion coating her tone with steel. "I want you to stop bothering me. No more letters, no more calls, no more flowers. Just go away!"

The hiss of an indrawn breath sounded in her ear. "It's because of him, isn't it? Your marriage has come between us—"

"There is no 'us'! Day has nothing to do with this." Panic edged into her voice as she realized this madman might be capable of anything, and that he might transfer his obsession to the man she loved.

"I'll never let you leave me again. Never!" Insanity rang clearly in the caller's voice in the instant before the receiver on the other end crashed down, making her yank the phone away from her ear with a wince.

In the shocking silence, she began to shiver convulsively; she wrapped her arms defensively around herself. He was close, she knew it. Too close. He sounded completely mad.

But she was sure she'd heard that voice before. But where? If she'd ever known him, it must have been just a casual encounter... perhaps a fan? To keep from screaming, she forced herself to concentrate on recalling the exact details of the conversation, not so much for its meaning, but as a way to identify him.

His speech was almost totally devoid of any accent that she could detect, which was odd in itself. In fact, he sounded almost as if he'd had lessons in elocution, much as she had in an effort to wipe out her Southwestern twang. Could he be an actor?

For the rest of the morning she went through all her leading men, all the behind-the-scenes assistants she could recall who had worked on the movies she'd made, but by the time lunch was on the table she was no closer to identifying the man. She simply couldn't picture any of the actors she knew doing something this sick. Besides, there had to be literally hundreds she didn't remember. Finally she decided it was hopeless. Odds were it was someone she'd never even met, someone who'd singled her out for reasons that only made sense to a sick mind.

After lunch, Beth Ann begged to go to the paddock and feed carrots to the horses that hadn't been ridden out. They were standing in the warm sun at the rails with one of the mares nuzzling Beth Ann's palm for more carrots when Angel heard hoofbeats. As she squinted in the bright light, her heart picked up its pace as she recognized Day riding toward them.

He was waving a large envelope at her. After reining in his mount, he vaulted out of the saddle and strode toward the paddock with the peculiar rolling gait only a man who spent most of his days on horseback could develop. She smiled at the sight, loving the way his lean hips shifted beneath the black leather chaps he wore. Then her attention was caught by his expression.

He was smiling, but not the cautious, guarded smile he'd turned on her so many times, and not the gentle, indulgent smile he bestowed upon his daughter. This smile verged on laughter—wide, full and exuberant. It made him so handsome he literally took her breath away, and she stopped stock-still as the force of his charisma hit her full force.

He swung the envelope in the air as he approached.

"What's got you so happy?" she inquired, feeling her own mood lighten.

He cupped her elbow and led her a little ways away from where Beth Ann was perched on the fence rails. "Good news," he said, his lips nearly brushing her ear.

A thrill of pure sexual anticipation raised goose bumps all over her arms and she chided herself for having such a one-track mind. "What good news?"

He flicked the edge of the envelope he'd been waving. "Custody papers. Signed, sealed and delivered." He laughed aloud, catching her to him and dancing her in a circle. "Nobody can ever take my little girl away from me now."

She was pleased for him, she really was. But a part of her registered with dismay his use of the singular words "my" and "me." Day wasn't thinking in terms of a partnership with her, that was clear. In his mind he was still a single father.

She knew her dreams were just that—dreams. Fantasies. But admitting that he didn't need her or want her for anything more than her body hurt deep in her heart. Shunting the hurt away, she plastered on a bright smile of her own. "That's great!" Stretching up, she aimed a kiss in the general direction of his cheek.

At the last moment, he turned his head and caught her mouth squarely with his own. "This calls for a celebration, and I have some ideas on exactly how we should go about it," he murmured.

"I like a man with ideas." She forced another smile. "This celebration could double as a farewell party."

His brow furrowed. "A farewell... Who's leaving?"

Taking a deep breath, she summoned her most reasonable tone. "I am. You only married me because you needed a wife for your custody battle. Now that you no longer have that to worry about, you don't need me anymore."

"But you can't leave." He sounded stunned, then almost angry. "I still need you."

She tried to smile, but her lips trembled at the edges and she pressed them together. "No, you don't." She touched the papers he still clutched in his hand. "You have what you need right here."

"What about Beth Ann?" He switched gears, hitting her in a spot only slightly less vulnerable than her love for him. "She's going to be shattered if you leave. She loves you."

"And I love her." *I love you, too. If you tell me you love me, even that you need my love, I'll stay.* "But we agreed to this marriage for reasons that would help each of us. We knew from the start it wasn't permanent."

His eyes had narrowed into slits of silver determination beneath the brim of his hat, and she saw a gleam in his eye that she didn't trust. "That's right," he said slowly. "Each of us was getting something out of this marriage. What about this guy who's after you? Where will you go if you leave? You won't be safe until he's caught."

He'd caught her unprepared, mirrored her own fears so exactly that she couldn't hide her expression.

Immediately his tone grew serious and commanding. He clasped her upper arms and rubbed his thumbs gently up and down her soft flesh. "What's wrong? Something else has happened, hasn't it? Did you get more flowers today?"

She shook her head, fixing her gaze on the studs fastening his shirt. "No." That wasn't a lie.

"Angel." He shook her lightly, then drew her in close to his strength. "Don't shut me out. What's wrong?"

The gentleness slipped under her resolve as nothing else could. She turned her head so that Beth Ann wouldn't see her face as tears of helplessness ran down her cheeks. "He called this morning."

"Called here?" His voice was incredulous.

She nodded as she drew back.

"What did he say?"

"H-he told me he'd see me soon—face-to-face. I got the impression that he's somewhere near here." She stopped, afraid to articulate her worst fears. "I have to leave."

"No!"

"Yes." She saw that he wasn't going to listen, and wearily she realized that she'd have to tell him everything. "He didn't just threaten me, Day. I told him to leave me alone and he got angry. It was as if he just snapped for a minute. He said that my marriage had come between us—" Her teeth began to chatter and she couldn't control the shivering again. "What if he tries to hurt you? Do you know how I'd feel if anything happened to you because of me?"

"How would you feel?" He gripped her shoulders, and his eyes were intense, searching.

"I would..." She couldn't go on, too unsure to say the words. Was he asking for her love? If only she knew. "I would never forgive myself," she finished. "You have to let me leave."

"You can't leave," he said again. "I need you. Beth Ann needs you." He pulled her into the comforting warmth of his arm and turned her toward the paddock. "You're staying. I'll call the sheriff right now, see if he's found out anything new, tell him what happened. Then I'll rearrange my schedule so I can work close to the house for a few days, keep a couple of the men here, too. If he's in the area, he'll surface soon and when he does, we'll be waiting for him."

She hesitated.

"Promise me you'll stay."

She watched Beth Ann skipping ahead of them, felt the strong, safe warmth of his arm protectively cast around her, and she knew she wasn't strong enough to deny herself a few more days with him. "I promise."

The next afternoon, he was out near the barn fixing the leaky faucet in the cattle yard when Corky started to bark. It was the sound the dog reserved for invaders on his territory and Day got to his feet and reached for the shotgun he was keeping with him all the time. A long white car came jouncing down the road from the main highway. By the time he got around to the front of the house it was rolling to a halt in a cloud of red dust.

After a moment, a short, dark-haired man elegantly attired in a natty gray summer suit climbed out from behind the wheel. Day positioned himself about five feet from the intruder, the gun crooked in a deceptively negligent manner in one arm.

"My good fellow—"

"We don't take to trespassers around here. Get your hands up." Day ignored the hand the man extended. Any man who wore a pink flower in his lapel any time but his wedding day was suspect for that reason alone. Elation began to burgeon within him. They'd put this guy away and Angel could quit worrying.

The man's smooth smile faltered as he responded to the barked command. "But I'm here to see Angelique—"

"Who will be delighted to see me escort you to the sheriff, I'm sure." Day jerked his head toward the man in a signal to two of his men who had come out of the barn. "Check him out, fellas."

As the two cowboys moved toward Gray Suit, he began to retreat. "Wait. There must be some mistake. I didn't tell her I was coming, but I'm sure she'll be glad to see me."

"Oh, I have no doubt of that."

The slamming of the front door prevented him from saying more.

"Day? What's going on?" Angel stopped and surveyed the way the cowhands were efficiently frisking their "guest."

When Day put out an arm, she stepped into it naturally. Gray Suit's eyes bulged. Day felt a satisfying sense of pride. She belonged to him, and it was obvious to anyone who looked. "I think our problem has just been solved."

Angel's eyebrows rose in puzzlement as she looked from Gray Suit to Day's shotgun and back again. "Why are you holding a gun on Karl?"

"You know him?"

"Of course. He's my agent." She started forward, but he held her back, anger making his words harsh.

"Did you tell him where you were?"

Realization began to dawn in her eyes. "Well, yes. But Karl couldn't possibly be the one stalking me. I would have recognized his voice."

"Not if he disguised it, altered it somehow."

"May I say something?" It was a plaintive request from the man Angel called her agent.

"Yes," Angel said.

"No." He'd always thought that expression about a man's finger "itching" to pull the trigger was just that: an expression. But believing that this man had been stalking Angel, threatening and frightening her after he'd wormed his way into her affections—his finger practically did itch to pull the trigger. Sobered by the thought, he eased it slightly away.

"I insist you listen to me for a moment." Gray Suit—Karl—wasn't a coward, whatever else he was. He gazed steadily into Day's eyes, though he must have been able to see the murderous intent he wasn't bothering to conceal. "I'm not the person you're after. Angel surely knows I would never, ever harm her."

"It's hard to know who to trust, Karl," Angel said. "How did you find me?"

The man dropped his hands and spread them in exasperation. "Since you gave me the address, all I had to do was ask for directions to the ranch at the local greasy spoon once I got into that little town a few miles back."

"Why didn't you call and let me know you were coming?"

The man's concerned expression matched his tone. "When I tried to call you this week, a machine picked up every time. I was worried about you. So here I am."

Angel snorted, but there was good humor in her voice. "The only worrying you've done, my dear barracuda, is whether or not you'll be able to con me into signing another contract."

"You wound me." Dramatically the man clapped a hand over his heart. Then his gaze moved from her to Day again. "So this cowboy is the reason you've squirreled yourself away in the desert. Care to make introductions, dear? I'd be delighted to meet your husband, which is another reason I'm here. Did you consider a prenuptial agreement? He could be after your money, you know."

"Coming from you, that's really funny." Angel was laughing as she walked toward Karl and linked her arm through his. "Day, he's harmless. Really. Let's all go inside and we can explain what's been going on to Karl."

Day wasn't nearly as convinced as she was, but the man looked and sounded sane—at least as sane as anyone else from L.A. And he wasn't about to leave her side for a minute, so she'd be safe enough.

Later that evening, he had to admit she'd been right. Karl Graines was no more a stalker than he was. And irritating though the man might be, he clearly cared about Angel in a paternal way that made Day forgive him even that damned lapel flower.

They talked him into staying for dinner, and while Angel excused herself to put Beth Ann to bed, Day learned that Karl had known about the letters and calls in L.A. The agent was horrified to learn that the contacts had continued at the ranch, and his concern for Angel was clear. When she left the living room later to bring in a plate of refreshments, Karl didn't waste any time.

"She's absolutely dead set against security, you know. Can you take care of her without help?"

Day nodded. "I think so. I have my men keeping their eyes open and the sheriff is still checking all over Deming."

Karl's shrewd eyes were worried. "This man sounds insanely determined. He could be dangerous to you and your employees, as well as to Angelique. Don't take any chances."

"Don't worry. I won't let him hurt my wife."

Karl smiled in a satisfied way that made Day wonder just what he was thinking. "I can see that." The smile faded and he eyed Day speculatively. "Angelique was made for the big screen, you know. Are you ever going to let her come back to the entertainment business?"

"The decision's not mine to make," he said stiffly. "When we married, Angel knew I wouldn't stop her from returning to her career if that's what she wants." Apparently Angel hadn't told her agent the true reasons they'd married. Well, he wasn't going to enlighten the man.

After Karl had climbed back into the long white car and driven away through the twilight, Day helped Angel clean up the kitchen. Then they went into the living room and sat before the fire he'd built in the baked adobe fireplace. They hadn't needed the warmth, but he'd wanted, for some reason, to impress Karl Graines with the atmosphere of his home.

The agent's last words echoed in his head. Did she want to go back? She hadn't appeared to miss her fast-paced life, but what did he know? The scripts she'd received in the mail haunted him. One of them lay on the coffee table right now. Had she chosen a new project? Was she going back to L.A. as soon as they'd caught the man who was threatening her life?

A gentle finger stroking his forehead startled him into jerking away from Angel's hand. She smiled at him. "You were looking pretty ferocious. What were you thinking about?"

He opened his mouth to make up some harmless fabrication as her fingers began to stroke through his hair. "I can't stand the idea of you leaving."

It was a toss-up which of them was more astonished.

Angel recovered first while he was still testing his tongue for more treachery, wondering if he dared try to say anything else. "I already promised you I wouldn't go anywhere until my overeager suitor is caught."

"You've been reading new scripts." He tried not to make it sound like an accusation. "Are you going to take on a new project?"

"I won't break my promise to you if that's what you're worrying about."

It was already too late for caution if he wanted her. "Dammit it, Angel, I'm not just talking about a few months. I want you to stay here for the rest of your life." He hurled the words at her like a challenge, rather than wooing her with sweet nothings as he should have.

"Why?" Her gaze was as wary as her voice.

"I've told you why. Beth Ann needs you."

Her face was still and thoughtful. He couldn't read her at all. Finally she said, "I don't think that's a good enough reason to base a marriage on."

"Not a good enough reason . . . ?" At last—a line he could pursue with certainty. He found his temper rising out of all proportion to her quiet words. "You don't think the fact that my daughter needs you, *loves* you, thinks of you as her mother now, is enough reason to continue our marriage?"

"It's important but I don't think—"

"You don't think what? Beth Ann will be devastated if you leave. You should reconsider before you abandon that little girl so easily."

Silence. He had to grit his teeth to keep from squirming; he felt like the ornery schoolboy he'd been as a youth when she subjected him to that thoughtfully probing gaze.

"Do you realize—" she wasn't quite smiling, but a hint of humor played around her lips "—that you fall back on that tired old line every time the topic of my leaving comes up?" Her voice heated with intensity. "When you first presented me with this marriage idea, you were very specific about its temporary nature, with the fact that eventually, you'd be wanting me to leave."

Sullenly, stubbornly, he got up and stood silent, caught in a web of his own words. Looking at the floor, he said, "It's never been for me . . . before . . . like it is with you."

"Great sex is not a good reason for two people to commit their lives to each other."

Was she deliberately misunderstanding him? "Great sex is only a part of it."

"What's the other part?"

Hell.

Why was she pushing him like this? He'd already told her he needed her. He started to reach for her but she was moving, snatching up the script that lay on the table before him. While he watched, speechless, she tossed the script into the fireplace in one quick, sure motion. Then she picked up the poker and stirred the slumbering embers to life.

Mesmerized, he watched the hungry tongues of flame embrace, then consume the thick sheaf of paper until it fell into remnants of useless ash. He turned disbelieving eyes to Angel. The implication of her action was too much for him to dare hope for.

"Wha—"

"That was a good script." She pointed a finger at the smoking embers. "And there are several more good ones in the study." She faced him with her chin up, defiant, and she'd never been lovelier to him than she was in that instant. "Once, not long ago, I'd have taken one, more than one of those projects, Day. But I don't want that life anymore."

He wanted to ask her what she did want, but his tongue felt too thick and clumsy to move. When she moved to stand before him, he could only stare at her, his heart thumping hard in his chest.

"I love you, Day." She took his right hand and placed it against the upper swell of her breast, and he could feel her heart beating. Her gaze was steady on his, and in her clear eyes, he saw a depth of feeling that staggered him. "Yes, I want to make our marriage permanent. Because I want to be Beth Ann's mother, but even more because I want to be your wife for the rest of my life."

Beneath his hand, her flesh was warm and soft. His head spun with the knowledge that she was *his!* Forever. The realization was sweet, indeed. His body began to react insistently to her nearness, urging him to claim her in that most basic, most elemental of possessions, and with a groan of need, he pulled her close, dropping his head to seek her lips.

She trembled against him as he took her mouth and traced all her soft, feminine contours. He felt hot and ready, so needy that his legs quivered, and before his knees could buckle he dragged her down to the buffalo-hide rug in front of the fireplace.

Tearing frantically at her clothing, then his own, he cast fabric aside until they were both naked. In one last moment of conscious thought, he reached for the small package of protection in his discarded wallet and donned it. Then he pulled her beneath him and covered her, surging forward in one glorious burst of power that sheathed him tightly within her.

She writhed beneath him, and a pang of remorse shot through him as he realized she hadn't been ready. Forcing himself to hold still, to resist the irresistible urge to thrust himself even deeper within her, he waited, waited, waited until her soft, secret flesh relaxed around him and the taut muscles in her legs signaled that she wasn't uncomfortable.

The afterglow from the fire warmed one side of his body as he began to move, drawing her legs up and up until they were folded beneath his chest, giving him a cradle for his upper body. She wrapped her arms around his back, and he felt her nails digging into his flesh. The sweet sting urged him into movement, and he began to rock steadily within her, the rhythmic thrust and retreat a glorious coiling spiral of excitement in her wet warmth.

He wanted it to last forever, but he could feel his body rushing out of control, urging him to spend himself within her. The little whimpers she was making told him that she was infected with the same fevered need he was. Her hips lifted, fell and lifted, over and over, faster and faster... and he was lost.

He buried his head in her neck as his rhythm disintegrated into a frantic maelstrom of movement. Her body received him as if fashioned for him and him alone. Her small noises gave way to great heaving gasps that echoed the buck and roll of her body beneath him. As his vision dimmed and his consciousness receded into a primitive, single-minded focus on fulfillment, he was vaguely aware of her body pulsing, clasping him as she achieved her own climax.

And then he knew nothing. Nothing, save for the sweet satisfaction of pouring himself into the woman he loved, giving himself totally to her until there was nothing more to give and he lay limp on her in complete satiation.

He wondered if he was crushing her. He ought to move. But her hands were gently stroking his back and he couldn't bring himself to break the small moment of contentment. Besides, he was so sleepy.... He turned his head and kissed her neck, thought again that he ought to move, but his muscles felt as if they weighed tons....

Eleven

Angel awoke five minutes before the alarm went off the next morning. Day was curled around her, one hand possessively spanning her hip as if, even in sleep, he would chain her to him.

There was no need, she thought with sad resignation. Her love bound her to him far more effectively than any chains ever would. His reaction—or more specifically, his lack of reaction—to her declaration of love last night, had withered any hope for happiness in her future. He hadn't said he loved her, though he was quick to point out that he needed her. While she didn't doubt that he desired her, she knew that without love it wouldn't be enough to hold them together.

By his silence, and by the way he had set out to deliberately sidetrack any further conversation, she could only interpret his behavior one way. Day was uncomfortable with her love. He didn't want it and he certainly didn't return it.

Hurt became a solid knot of anguish in her chest, and she slipped quietly from his slumbering embrace. After dressing, she went to the kitchen to begin the morning routine. By the time Day entered the kitchen ten minutes later, she was in the dining room laying the table for breakfast. She lingered for a moment, drawing a deep breath when she heard his booted steps. She had to be calm when she faced him. Letting him see how his rejection had hurt wouldn't accomplish anything except further humiliation.

"Angel?" His deep voice called out to her. Before she could respond, he strode into the dining room. "I didn't get a chance to—"

A shot rang out from somewhere near the house, cutting off his words and shocking them both into silence. A second later, the shouting of the men galvanized them into action.

Day turned and ran for the back door. "Stay in here," he ordered over his shoulder.

She didn't bother arguing. But as he slammed through the door, she was right on his heels. Wes came puffing up, moving faster than she'd ever seen a man in cowboy boots run. "Boss! Somebody was in the barn last night. Three of the mares are gone!"

Day swore. "Saddle up, everybody."

To Angel, one thing seemed vitally important. She caught Wes's sleeve as he turned. "Did you see anyone?"

"Naw." Behind him, the other hands were already leading more mounts out. "Soon's I saw the barn doors were open, I fired a shot to bring everybody out here pronto. Them thieves could be in the next state by now."

Day had wheeled at the sound of her voice. "Get back to the house and stay there. This could be the work of your admirer, and I don't want you exposed."

The tone of his voice, more than the curt words, made her dig in her heels when he tried to push her toward the door. "I'll go back to the house," she said, "but only because I don't want Beth Ann to wake up and find us both gone. Just because I told you I loved you doesn't mean you own me."

His grip tightened, and for a second, some fierce expression she couldn't interpret flashed across his face. He dragged her toward him and she gasped when her body came up against his. He lowered his head and pressed a rough kiss on her mouth, then laughed when she tried to turn her head and shove him away.

Effortlessly he subdued her struggles. "Oh, I own you, baby, make no mistake," he said. "Body and soul, you're mine. And you always will be."

"Ready, Boss?"

He released her and gave her a push in the direction of the porch. "Stay here. You and I have some talking to do when I get back."

Watching him ride out, she suddenly felt more vulnerable and alone than she had since she arrived at the ranch. She whistled for Corky, but the black-and-white dog didn't come running. Darned contrary animal. He was always underfoot except when you needed him, Day said, and she was beginning to think he was right. Then a thought struck her. What if whoever took the horses had killed Corky? She couldn't believe the contrary old canine would stand quietly and allow someone to lead three mares away. Her heart sank. She was fond of the perverse creature.

She went back inside and put away the unused breakfast things. The men would be starving when they returned, but she wouldn't know whether to feed them breakfast, lunch or dinner until they came back. Horse thieves. She couldn't believe they'd come so close to the house! Reaction set in, and as she replaced boxes of cereal in the pantry, her hands began to shake.

She linked them together and squeezed until her wedding band cut into her flesh. Then she realized that Day had ridden out so fast he hadn't had a chance to call the sheriff, so she did.

"I'll be out as soon as I can get away," he promised. "Don't let anyone disturb the barn area. There might be prints or tracks we can lift. If Day comes back, tell him to stay put until we talk."

It wasn't until after she'd hung up the receiver that she realized she'd completely forgotten to ask him if he'd made any progress finding out who was after her. Oh, well. Right now they had bigger things to worry about.

Beth Ann awoke an hour later and she fed her breakfast, grateful for the child's constant chatter that kept her fears at bay. As she was surveying the contents of the big freezer, trying to decide what to thaw for the evening meal, she heard the unmistakable sound of a car coming up the ranch road.

"Angel! Somebody's coming!" Beth Ann's excited voice confirmed it.

She closed the freezer and walked through the house and onto the front porch, shading her eyes for a better view in the too-bright day. She'd hoped that it was Karl again, but this car was a smaller sedan in a dusty dark blue. Probably a salesman, she thought.

As the car rolled to a halt, she walked out to meet the dark-haired man just visible behind the wheel. He must have missed the No Soliciting sign posted at the main highway. If the guy was lucky, she could send him on his way before Day saw him. Day's impatience with salesmen approached dangerous proportions sometimes.

"Hello," she said as the man stepped from the car.

"Hello." He was tall and slender, soft voiced, with a carefully knotted tie and large reflective sunglasses hiding his eyes from the fierce desert sun.

She smiled, puzzled when he didn't state his purpose for being on the ranch. "You must have missed the sign."

"No." He smiled back. "I didn't have any trouble finding the ranch."

"Oh, I didn't realize—" She stopped, more than a little confused. Day hadn't mentioned inviting company today. "I thought you were a salesman."

His smile faded. "Angelique. Don't you recognize me?" The wattage in his smile increased again. "It must be the glasses," he said, reaching up and removing them.

The moment she heard him utter her name, she knew. Time slowed and stopped, and for a moment she honestly thought she might swoon, the world swirling and whirling around her until everything faded into black.

But she didn't. As he took off the glasses, she took deep, fortifying breaths. Oh, God. She did know him! Though she never would have remembered him in three lifetimes if she hadn't seen him again. He was the man who had tried to get her number from Karl several weeks ago!

What was his name...Jared? Jason? No, Janson. That was it. Janson Brand. A stage name if she'd ever heard one. He'd been an extra in the first film she'd ever done, the one that had started her career, and she'd gone out with him once, maybe twice. As memory returned, so did understanding. He'd grown up in Las Cruces, he'd told her, and she'd been so homesick for New Mexico and so pleased to meet someone from close to home that she'd told him of her early life around Deming. No wonder he'd been able to find her so easily. He was one of the few people in the world who knew where she'd come from. He must have guessed she'd come back here when she vanished—she'd probably even told him Dulcie was her best friend when they were trading "did-you-knows" and "do-you-remembers" all those years ago.

Uncomfortably she remembered how intense he'd been, how crushed, when she'd decided not to go out with him anymore. She'd still been too raw from her failed marriage and losing Emmie to be looking for a serious relationship. As soon as she'd realized that he was beginning to consider her more than just a friend, she'd backed away.

With a start, she realized he was waiting expectantly for her response. Fear rose in her. She couldn't imagine this man writing those horrible letters, but he must have. Heaven only knew what was going on in his head.

"Janson!" she said. "How nice to see you. How have you been?"

His expression clouded momentarily. "All right."

If she treated him normally, courteously, perhaps he'd respond in kind. She could invite him in for coffee and keep him there until the sheriff arrived. Keeping her voice carefully friendly, she asked, "What have you been doing with yourself since I last saw you? A list of credits a mile long, I'll bet."

"No," he said slowly, and she could almost see him wilting. "Actually, work has been rather difficult to find. I've never . . . hit it big like you did."

She didn't know what to say. Once they'd both been young unknowns. He still was. "There's still plenty of time," she offered gently. "Your big break is probably right around the corner."

"I hope so." She found the way he brightened again somehow pathetic. "And won't it be wonderful to share our successes together, darling?"

She froze. His voice was far too intimate. "But, Janson, you know I'm married now—"

"You can get a divorce." His voice rang with impatience. "I've waited so long to be with you. I can't wait any longer. Are you ready to go?"

The jarring switch from reality to . . . to whatever he was thinking had her fumbling for a reply. "Go? I can't go anywhere." She gestured to Beth Ann, who had come forward and was hovering at her side peering out at Janson. "I have a child to take care of now."

"We have to go." Out of nowhere, it seemed, he produced a sleek black pistol. As he waved it at her, a huge ball of fear expanded in her stomach.

Automatically she shoved Beth Ann behind her.

"Come along, Angelique. We'll have to take the child along, I suppose."

"No, wait!" Her brain was racing ahead, examining all the angles of this bizarre turn of events. It was clear that Janson Brand had been the one stalking her all this time, just as it was becoming increasingly obvious that he wasn't rational. At least, not about her.

If Beth Ann went with them, she was afraid he might turn on the child as he thought more about the relationship between Angel and Day. She couldn't allow him to hurt Beth Ann.

"Look," she said desperately, "she'll get in our way. Besides, if I take her, her father will be sure to come after us. It would be better to leave her here."

"All right, but hurry." He turned his wrist and checked his watch. Dull sparks of light shot off the surface of the dark pistol. "We're already late."

Late for what? Terrified and praying that Beth Ann wouldn't realize it, she snatched up the little girl and hurried to the porch. Setting her on the steps, she took Beth Ann's face between her hands, hoping against hope that the child could absorb everything she was going to say. "Beth Ann, listen carefully. I need you to be a very big girl for Daddy and me right now."

The child's eyes were wide. "Dat man has a gun."

Angel nodded. "I know. Listen. I'm going to get in the car and go away with that man. As soon as you can't see the car anymore, you run out to the fire bell—" she wanted to point to the tall pole on which the fire bell was mounted but she didn't dare "—and ring that bell until Daddy comes home. He'll come fast when he hears the bell. Tell

Daddy that the man took me and that he has a gun and that we're in a blue car. Can you do that?''

Beth Ann nodded, her small face pinched. Her lower lip began to tremble. "But I don't want you to—"

"I have to! I don't want to but that bad man is making me go." She kissed the child and stood. "Run and ring the bell as soon as you can't see the car anymore, okay?''

Beth Ann nodded again. "Okay."

"Good girl!" Angel was already turning and walking back toward the blue car. Janson was waiting, the pistol held casually in one hand as he opened her door with an old-fashioned courtesy that didn't match the gun's menace.

Surely there had to be a way to get that gun. Everything she'd ever learned warned her not to get in that car and go with him. Then she'd be at his mercy.

But if she didn't, he might hurt Beth Ann.

Day was miles away on the range when he heard the fire bell. They'd found the mares a while back, loose on the range. Puzzling. It almost made him think they'd gotten out by accident, but he didn't know of any way a horse could open the barn doors.

They'd rounded up the mares and started back toward the house. Then, twenty minutes ago, one of the men had discovered Corky, drugged and tied to a cottonwood tree near the wash.

His heart had nearly stopped when he'd realized the implications of that find. Leaving one of the men to bring the barely conscious dog home across his saddle, Day had wheeled his horse and started back for the house as fast as he'd dared.

Whoever had taken the horses hadn't wanted them. All he'd wanted to do was create a diversion. And once Corky had been put out of action, there was absolutely nothing to stop him from coming right into the house after Angel.

He couldn't ever remember being so terrified in his entire life, not even when he'd thought he might really lose Beth Ann.

Beth Ann! His child was with Angel. Unprotected. As he raced for the house, the fire bell began to ring, and after that first terrible moment of understanding what the noise was, he began to curse steadily, outrage and anger building inside him with every hoofbeat.

He'd kill anyone who tried to harm the woman and child he loved.

He was wild-eyed when he finally rode into the yard. Spotting Beth Ann holding the long rope on the fire bell, her little body jerking as she pulled, he dismounted before his horse had come to a halt and scooped her into his arms. Relief made his muscles weak as he clutched her to him.

"Where's the fire, filly?" He was straining his eyes for smoke, sniffing for the telltale odor, and it was a minute before he realized Angel was nowhere to be seen. Beth Ann was shuddering and crying in his arms, and he had to take precious moments to calm her down before he could understand what she was trying to tell him.

"N-n-no fire, D-daddy. A b-b-bad man taked A-a-angel away." Tears rolled down her chubby cheeks and she gasped between sobs, "Wif a g-g-g-gun."

His entire body went still. This was beyond his worst nightmare. "What did the man look like, Beth Ann? Can you remember anything about what he was wearing or his hair color?"

"H-he had a blue car." Beth Ann sobbed again and he rubbed her back soothingly. "Angel said she didn't w-want to go and she told me to ring the b-b-bell 'til you comed."

He carried her with him, wrapped around his neck like a monkey, as he ran inside to call the sheriff, only to find the man was already on his way to the ranch, thanks to a call from Angel earlier in the morning. In a few terse sentences, he explained what had happened to the dispatcher, who promised to call for reinforcements.

In a few more minutes, the yard was filled with men and horses. He stood on the hood of his truck and told them what he knew, then prepared to leave. Joe-Bob and Smokey were going to follow in a second truck, while Wes would stay and supervise the rest of the hands and care for Beth Ann.

When he handed her to Wes with a last kiss, she began to scream and beg him not to leave her. She was too little and too scared to understand that he had no choice, he thought grimly. As he gunned the engine and raced down the lane, her little voice rose to a frantic shriek. "Da-a-a-ad-deeee!"

Leaving his traumatized child behind was one of the hardest things he'd ever had to do in his life. It ranked right up there with setting out to find his wife, fearing she might be dead at the hands of a madman already.

Janson Brand talked the whole way down the bumpy road to the main highway.

Angel barely heard a word he said. All her attention was focused on that ugly black pistol he clutched in his right hand as he gripped the wheel. How to get that gun away from him? Her mind raced, but no incredibly brilliant solutions appeared.

Twice they stopped at cattle gates and he asked her to open them. She could practically feel the intensity of his interest directed at her as she got out of the car and opened the heavy gates, then closed them behind the car again after he pulled through. The urge to run was so strong she nearly couldn't resist it, but she beat it back.

There was no place to run out here. The land was so flat he could see her for miles. Even if she did manage to get away from him, up to where the land sloped into rolling hills, she'd have to be found fast or she'd die without water.

She was still working on that problem when they came to the third and final gate. There was a sparse scattering of cattle nearby. With a start, she recognized Old Red, the dangerous bull Day had cautioned her about time after time. She opened her mouth to warn Janson, then caught herself and shut it again.

How could she use the bull's dislike of humans to her advantage? He'd kill her if she got out of the car. *And Janson might kill you if you don't. Some choice.*

"Angelique, would you please open the gate?" His voice was courteous and pleasant, but she'd already learned that he would shift into a frighteningly unstable fury if she challenged him. With the fingers of her right hand, she cradled her left forearm. He'd grabbed it in a blind rage minutes ago when she'd tried to reason with him once again. She knew there were going to be marks.

The only good thing was that he seemed to forget almost instantly that she was his prisoner. In whatever fantasy he inhabited, she was with him because she loved him.

And she'd better not forget it.

"Angelique!" His voice had risen and she jumped. When he went on, the fracture in his smooth tones warned her he would explode again if she wasn't careful. "I asked you to open the gate."

"But, Janson, I'm afraid." She didn't know what else to say.

He laughed, not unkindly. "It's a good thing I'm taking you away from ranching, if you're afraid of cows. They're harmless."

"Not that bull." She hesitated, then seized the only excuse she could think of, the only thing that might help her now. "That bull hates women. Everyone on the Red Arrow knows it." If he knew much about cattle, she was sunk. No bull she'd ever heard of could tell a man from a woman if the woman wasn't wearing skirts.

"He hates women?" Janson repeated.

"He'll go after a woman every time, but he won't bother men," she elaborated. Was he swallowing this or was he going to break out in another one of those maniacal rages? A trickle of sweat rolled down her temple, despite the air-conditioning cooling the interior of the car.

Janson appeared to think that over. Then he shrugged. "I guess I'll have to open this gate, then, won't I? You're too precious to risk."

Her whole body felt shaky with relief as he put the car in park with the engine idling, then opened his door and stepped out. When she saw that he was taking the gun, her heart sank even though she'd expected it. As soon as he was out of earshot, she unclipped her seat belt.

Old Red was on the far side of the car from the driver's door and he didn't see Janson immediately. But as the man cleared the vehicle's hood and strode toward the gate, the bull snorted and pawed the ground.

Janson's head swung toward the bull, then back to the car, and she could see the uncertainty and dawning fear in his face. It was now or never.

She lunged across the seat, fumbling for the automatic gearshift and shoving it into reverse at the same instant that she slammed her left foot down onto the pedal. As the car picked up speed, she righted herself in the seat, transferred her right foot to the gas and grabbed for the door handle.

Janson was screaming and running toward her, but he couldn't run fast enough to catch the car as she lurched backward. And coming at him, faster than anyone would ever believe, was Old Red. Turning the wheel, she veered into a sharp backward turn, slammed on the brake and started forward, flooring it on the road back to the ranch.

A shot rang out and she ducked reflexively but didn't slow her speed. A quick check in the rearview mirror, however, showed her that Janson wasn't shooting at her. He'd gone down on one knee and was aiming straight at the raging bull surging toward him.

She averted her eyes, unable to bear the thought of Old Red dying because of her.

Day was a little more than halfway out the ranch road, driving like a bat out of hell, when he saw a cloud of dust in the distance. It quickly resolved itself into a blue sedan, driving a whole lot faster than was safe or comfortable on the rutted road.

Without hesitation, he braked the pickup, grabbing his rifle and opening the door in one smooth motion. Vaulting into the bed of the truck, he braced the gun on the roof and sighted down the barrel. *Give me a reason to kill you, mister.*

As the blue car approached, it slowed. He lined up the cross hairs on the driver's door as the car skidded to a halt. "Get out and get your hands up!"

Sunlight bounced off the windshield, hiding whoever was inside. Slowly the door began to open. A blond head appeared, and with dawning incredulity, he realized he had Angel squarely in his sights. He damn near jumped down and ran toward her before he remembered that the man might be hiding in the car.

"Walk over here if you can," he called to her. "Are you alone?"

Her eyes focused on him and she nodded. She took a step, then another, and as he watched, slowly dropped to her knees in the dusty road.

He did race to her then, his heart pounding with fear. Had the guy shot her? Was she bleeding? The second he reached her, he began to run his hands over her in a frantic quest for her injuries. "Where is he? What did he do to you?" It occurred to him that he didn't even know *who* had taken her. "Do you know him?"

She raised her head, catching his hands and holding them still. "I'm not hurt. His name is Janson Brand. I met him, dated him a couple of times while I was doing my first film." She shrugged, but her lower lip trembled and he could see she wasn't as unmoved as she wanted him to believe. "He's...not sane. All these months...it was him."

He had a hell of a lot of questions, but most of them could wait. "Where is he now?"

Her gaze clouded. "I told him Old Red hated women, so he got out to open the gate. I think—I think he shot the bull. He had a pistol. If he hitched a ride, he might be gone."

He stared at her. The abrupt realization that he hadn't lost her was too much and he put his arms around her and pulled her to him, just needing to feel her against him. "My God, woman, I thought..." He let his voice trail away, unable to articulate everything he'd feared.

The sound of vehicles approaching from both directions interrupted him, and he helped her carefully to her feet. She didn't appear to be hurt, though she winced when he grasped her forearm. Rolling up the sleeve of her blouse, he could see already-purpling splotches the size of fingertips.

The thought of that man putting his hands on her made him so furious he could barely speak, but all the same, he was damned glad that was all she had to show in the way of reminders from her harrowing experience.

The first vehicle to roll to a halt was the other truck from the ranch, bringing first-aid supplies and the additional weapons he'd ordered them to get. The two men were hardly out of the truck, exclaiming over Angel, when the sheriff pulled up from the other direction.

Joe-Bob had gotten Angel to sit down and was giving her a drink from a canteen. Day walked over to meet the sheriff, wanting a word with the man without Angel over-hearing.

"Day." The lawman's nod was short and serious. "We got another problem out by the main road. You know anything about it?"

Day scratched his head. "Maybe. You know the guy who took Angel at gunpoint while I was out tracking the mares? I called your office about it a little while ago."

The sheriff nodded. "Right. The dispatcher radioed me, told me your wife had been abducted. What's happened?"

"Angel got away from him out near the main road," Day explained. "She left him shooting at one of my best bulls. Did he kill him?"

Slowly the sheriff shook his head. "Depends on who you're asking about. That big red bull of yours is standing over something in the front pasture that looks an awful lot like the remains of a human being. I have one of my deputies guarding him from a cruiser—remembered that bull ain't too friendly to people." The sheriff looked past him for a moment, at the woman sipping from Joe-Bob's canteen. "She's a lucky lady. Did you know the fella?"

Day nodded. "She did. She worked with him once. Apparently he'd had her on his mind for quite a while." He hesitated. "Can we finish this later? I know you'll want to talk to Angel, but I'd really like to get her back to the house. We left our daughter there with the rest of my men. She needs to know her mama's okay."

The sheriff gave him a sympathetic nod. "There's no rush. Send some of your hands out here with a tranquilizer gun when you get back. I already called the coroner, but I don't particularly want any more bodies for him to identify."

The coroner and the medic team had left, taking with them Janson Brand's trampled body. The sheriff had come back and gone again. As the evening sun set behind the mountains to the west, all the excitement seemed to have passed.

Angel paused in the door of the living room and Day looked up from the couch and smiled. "Is she asleep?"

She sighed. "Finally." Beth Ann hadn't wanted Angel out of her sight since they'd returned to the house in late morning. It would take a while for the child to feel safe again, she was sure. Fortunately, with Day having sole custody, Beth Ann would have all the time she needed. Angel smiled. "I guess we'll worry about weaning her away from the blanket again in a few months."

"I'm glad it makes her feel more secure." Day didn't smile. "I wish I had something that would make me feel better."

Guilt rose in her and she perched on the couch beside him. "Day, I'm sorry. After all your warnings, I should never have gone out to meet that car. I just didn't think—"

He put an arm around her, pulling her down across his lap. "It wasn't your fault. If he hadn't succeeded today, he'd still be out there. Besides—" he grimaced "—I shouldn't have ridden off this morning. My men could have tracked those mares without me. I wasn't thinking of your safety like I should have been."

She smiled, linking her arms around his neck. "Have you got a coin? Heads, I take the blame. Tails, it's all yours."

He chuckled. "You've made your point. I won't talk about blame anymore if you won't." He heaved a sigh. "I'm just glad it's over."

Angel sobered. "So am I, although I feel guilty saying that aloud when poor Janson is dead."

"Poor Janson, my a—"

Her palm cut off his words. "He must have been very sick. I can't blame him, either."

He could, but for the sake of harmony, he'd drop it. Still, when he imagined how terrified she must have been...

"What are you thinking about?" She traced a finger across the weathered lines in his forehead, smoothing the frown away.

He hesitated. Then he reached up and captured her hands, holding them pressed against his heart. "I was thinking about what you told me last night. Today, when I realized he had you, I was scared to death I'd never get to hold you like this again." He took a deep breath and looked into her eyes. "I love you, Angel Kincaid. I want you to be my wife for the rest of our lives together."

Her brown eyes were soft with love, shining with emotion. "Oh, Day, I love you, too. This is what I want, cowboy. Not fame, not money, not awards. Just you, and Beth Ann, and any other children we have together."

A great weight lifted from his heart. He hadn't realized how badly he'd needed to hear her say exactly that. Gathering her into his embrace, he kissed her with all the pent-up passion she aroused in him. When she was boneless and breathless in his arms, he raised his head a fraction. Against her lips, he asked, "And how soon do you want to start producing these brothers and sisters for our daughter?"

She wriggled on his lap, just a little. "Feels to me as if we could fire up the production line tonight."

He laughed aloud, enjoying her daring. "No doubt about it, darlin'." He lifted her into his arms and stood effortlessly, starting up the stairs toward their bedroom. "The sooner we get started, the more years we'll have to enjoy the results of our labor."

She echoed his laughter. "Well, then, in the interests of saving time, let's get started."

He stopped halfway up the stairs, his smile fading, his gaze intense as it met hers. "Together."

She touched her lips to his in a silent pledge of her love. "Together."

* * * * *

SILHOUETTE® *Desire®*

COMING NEXT MONTH

Take 4 bestselling love stories FREE

Plus get a FREE surprise gift!

Special Limited-time Offer

Mail to Silhouette Reader Service™

3010 Walden Avenue
P.O. Box 1867
Buffalo, N.Y. 14269-1867

YES! Please send me 4 free Silhouette Desire® novels and my free surprise gift. Then send me 6 brand-new novels every month, which I will receive months before they appear in bookstores. Bill me at the low price of $2.44 each plus 25¢ delivery and applicable sales tax, if any.* That's the complete price and a savings of over 10% off the cover prices—quite a bargain! I understand that accepting the books and gift places me under no obligation ever to buy any books. I can always return a shipment and cancel at any time. Even if I never buy another book from Silhouette, the 4 free books and the surprise gift are mine to keep forever.

225 BPA ANRS

Name	(PLEASE PRINT)	
Address	Apt. No.	
City	State	Zip

This offer is limited to one order per household and not valid to present *Silhouette Desire®* subscribers. *Terms and prices are subject to change without notice.
Sales tax applicable in N.Y.

UDES-295   ©1990 Harlequin Enterprises Limited

He's Too Hot To Handle...but she can take a little heat.

SILHOUETTE

Summer Sizzlers

This summer don't be left in the cold, join Silhouette for the hottest Summer Sizzlers collection. The perfect summer read, on the beach or while vacationing, Summer Sizzlers features sexy heroes who are "Too Hot To Handle." This collection of three new stories is written by bestselling authors Mary Lynn Baxter, Ann Major and Laura Parker.

Available this July wherever Silhouette books are sold.

Coming in June from

SILHOUETTE®

Desire®

FROM HERE TO MATERNITY

DR. DADDY
by Elizabeth Bevarly

The latest in her series celebrating the unexpected
joys of motherhood—and fatherhood!

Feisty redhead Zoey Holland thought Dr. Jonas
Tate was stubborn, sullen and way too serious! It
wasn't until the doctor asked Zoey for advice
raising his niece that she realized he was also
unbelievably sexy!

FROM HERE TO MATERNITY: Look what the stork
brought—a bundle of joy and the promise of love!

A new series from Nancy Martin

Who says opposites don't attract?

Three sexy bachelors
should've seen trouble coming
when each meets a woman
who makes his blood boil—
and not just because she's beautiful....

In March—
THE PAUPER AND THE PREGNANT PRINCESS (#916)

In May—
THE COP AND THE CHORUS GIRL (#927)

In September—
THE COWBOY AND THE CALENDAR GIRL

Watch the sparks fly as these handsome hunks fall for
the women they swore they didn't want!
Only from Silhouette Desire.

OA

**In June, get ready for thrilling romances
and FREE BOOKS—Western-style—
with...**

WESTERN *Lovers*

You can receive the first 2 Western Lovers titles FREE!

June 1995 brings Harlequin and Silhouette's
WESTERN LOVERS series, which combines larger-than-
life love stories set in the American West! And WESTERN
LOVERS brings you stories with your favorite themes...
"Ranch Rogues," "Hitched In Haste," "Ranchin' Dads,"
"Reunited Hearts" the packaging on each book
highlights the popular theme found in each WESTERN
LOVERS story!

And in June, when you buy either of the Men Made In
America titles, you will receive a WESTERN LOVERS title
absolutely FREE! Look for these fabulous combinations:

♦ Buy ALL IN THE FAMILY
  by Heather Graham Pozzessere (Men Made In
  America) and receive a FREE copy of
  BETRAYED BY LOVE by Diana Palmer
  (Western Lovers)

♦ Buy THE WAITING GAME
  by Jayne Ann Krentz (Men Made In America)
  and receive a FREE copy of
  IN A CLASS BY HIMSELF by JoAnn Ross
  (Western Lovers)

**Look for the special, extra-value shrink-wrapped
packages at your favorite retail outlet!**

HARLEQUIN® ▼ *Silhouette*®

Announcing
the New Pages & Privileges™ Program
from Harlequin® and Silhouette®

Get All This FREE
With Just One Proof-of-Purchase!

- **FREE Hotel Discounts** of up to 60% off at leading hotels in the U.S., Canada and Europe

- **FREE Travel Service** with the guaranteed lowest available airfares plus 5% cash back on every ticket

- **FREE $25 Travel Voucher** to use on any ticket on any airline booked through our Travel Service

- **FREE Petite Parfumerie** collection (a $50 Retail value)

- **FREE Insider Tips Letter** full of fascinating information and hot sneak previews of upcoming books

- **FREE Mystery Gift** (if you enroll before June 15/95)

And there are more great gifts and benefits to come!
Enroll today and become Privileged!
(see insert for details)
